Alexander King and the Secret Society of the Archons

by Niels Lauersen

Published by Legacy Press Books
A subsidiary of S & P Productions, Inc.
311 Main Street, Suite D
El Segundo, CA 90245
310-640-8885
www.legacypressbooks.com

Published and Printed in the United States of America

ISBN: 978-1-950326-55-6

A Tribute

Niels died weeks before the publication of this book. He was my friend for over fifty years. He was one of a kind, who loved life and lived it to the fullest. A very private person who gave endlessly to those in need. A humanitarian who never asked for anything. I will always love him and miss him. Niels was a very special soul whose eternal light will shine forever.

He wrote two books for young people, that were very different from the dozen books he wrote throughout his professional life; another proof of his love for children. We will honor his life by committing to publishing them all.

Phyllis Keitlen
Founder/President
Savvy/Chic, Inc. dba SoChicNYC

TABLE OF CONTENTS

PREFACE

Biography

PREFACE

It was an unusually calm night in Fredericks Port; the star-filled sky sparkled like diamonds as the sun began its descent over the horizon. A stretched Yellow Mercedes Benz limousine moved slowly towards Mole Drive and came to a sudden stop on Heaven Road.

The driver, dressed in an immaculate black suit, bright white shirt, black tie, high black boots, white gloves, and a shiny black chauffeur's cap, stepped onto the sidewalk. He opened the back door and bowed to the passenger, a tall elegant gentleman, who climbed out. The passenger wore an impressive bowler hat, his black suit sat well on his striking physique, and his black shoes shone in the starlight.

The chauffeur handed him an antique cane with the head of an eagle carved into its handle, and a large package wrapped in old faded newspapers, on which sat an envelope.

The man walked to Mole Drive and turned right, each step echoing like the boots with their steel reinforced heels worn by the Honor Guards who protect the Tomb of the Unknown Soldier.

The street shook with each step… 'Smack-Smack-Smack-Smack'… and his cane made 'Bang' 'Bang' sounds each time its tip hit the pavement.

The street shook until the man reached Nine Mole Road.

'Smack-Smack-Smack-Smack' - 'Bang'

'Smack-Smack-Smack-Smack' - 'Bang'

Number Nine, a small white Dutch Colonial house, faced the street. A white picket fence circled the house and two white columns seemed to hold up its roof. A rusty old brown '9' hung from a nail on the right column.

He stepped up to the front door and found a paper with SLEUTHER HOLMESBY tacked on it. Nervously the man bit his lip as he studied the house.

Sleuther Holmesby was a former super global spy who also had a Luxemburg address that he rarely used. He was of British descent and had been a spy, a mole, and an undercover agent for several countries. He was a man of the world but had left his sleuthing activities suddenly and moved to Fredericks Port where he had gone incognito, but he had never lost his secret 'mole' powers.

Fredericks Port itself had been an important shipping town with its booming steel factories. Then the steel industry faded, the factories collapsed, and Fredericks Port became a ghost town, a no-man's land.

The landfill next to the river was turned into a prison complex, but the air smelled as if rotten meat had permeated outside the perimeter of the jail's fence. The entire area was encased in smog and the jail was referred to as a death camp that few prisoners were seen to leave. The government called it a rehabilitation prison used to transform bad people into angels, but everyone knew that people died there under mysterious circumstances.

The east side of Fredericks Port, however, flourished as a collection of boarding schools, high schools, colleges, and a university, and the hills to the north housed a residential, bedroom community, where the teachers, writers, journalists, prison guards, and sleuths lived. Mole Drive cut through this neighborhood.

The elegant gentleman looked at the envelope on the package in his hands and confirmed that it was addressed to 'Sleuther Holmesby, Nine Mole Drive, Fredericks Port'. He dropped the packet next to the door with a big hollow sound, 'Ba-Boom!' then turned to leave.

'Smack-Smack-Smack-Smack' – 'Bang'.

'Smack-Smack-Smack-Smack' - 'Bang' was heard all the way down Mole Drive. He marched back down the stairs swinging his cane up into the air then banged it against the sidewalk. The driver opened the car door and the man stepped into the Stretch. The Yellow Limo then drove up Heaven Road as silently as it had arrived.

Sleuther Holmesby was awakened by the wild noises outside, and jumped out of bed. He slept comfortably in blue Bermuda shorts and a white T-shirt emblazoned in red letters with 'The Democracy of China'. He was a staunch supporter of a movement to turn China into a democratic society.

Staying close to the wall and away from the window he slowly parted the curtains and peeking out, caught site of the man in the bowler hat marching up to a Stretched Mercedes Benz. He watched as the car drove away across Mole Drive and up Heaven Road.

Detective Holmesby put on a long robe and his favorite old faded red baseball cap, and went out to retrieve the packet. He opened the letter addressed to him and read:

ATTENTION MY FELLOW WORLDIANS

and

ALL ITS BRIGHT KIDS.

TOP SECRET FOR YOUR EYES ONLY!!

This book contains classified information that is not to be shared with anyone.

I am the only PERSON ALIVE TODAY who has cracked the secret code to the Golden World "UTROVIA".

This is the world we dream about; a world where all people live in balance, in harmony, peace, prosperity, wealth, well-being, and happiness.

This is a Wonder World; a brave new world, where people have achieved great wisdom. It is a world with the most advanced technologies and wonder drugs that with our current knowledge would have taken us hundreds of years to achieve.

It is a rich and powerful world. Its people have been controlling everything in the universe… everything and more. They even decide who wins wars on earth and in the stars.

Without knowing it Alexander was taken to this amazing Paradise but as you will learn, he is not yet aware of it. The "Delta-Eyes" who are super leaders and super spies from Utrovia have sent for him to engage in a highly secret mission. One day they might send for one of you bright kids to perform another secret mission; one that will benefit the world.

You must tell no one about this Golden World or try to find the Golden Paradise… or you could end up in the Skull-and-Bone cemetery!

I will continue to share with you the codes I break and what I am learning about this new awesome world.

This must remain our secret!

Professor T.G. Rotcod, Universal Super Spy

The international super spy Sleuther Holmesby was well aware of the brilliant, brave and intelligent Archons and their work to eliminate all the evil Nikons, the devilish dictators and their terrorists who are trying to destroy our planet. He was expecting this packet and knew he had to get this information to all the smart and brave men, women and children, who have been preparing to fight for honor and truth.

He knew he had to keep this information top secret, and he knew how to help Professor T.G Rotcod and the brilliant Archons lead the World into an awesome, peaceful and sustainable democracy once again.

Sleuther Holmesby had a look of determination on his face as he read T.G. Rotcod's letter, then he picked up the newspaper-wrapped secret packet. Looking around to make sure he wasn't being watched, he walked back inside his house, sat down at his kitchen table, and began the painstaking work to break the liberation code.

The Haunted House

The wind howled around the old wooden house. Alexander tossed and turned in bed. The sheets were wrapped tightly around his legs making them impossible to move. It had been an unusually hot September day so the window was open to allow for some cool breeze. But now he was cold, and his snoring came in gasps. The large grandfather clock in the corner showed an hour before midnight but his snoring drowned out the clock's tick-tocking. Suddenly a huge gust of wind crashed into his room like a tornado. It unhooked the tiny metal latch on his window causing the shutters to smack the window with a booming whack! Alexander woke up and thought what a wicked night it was… Was someone or something sending him a message?

He jolted upright in bed. His young pale body shook as he watched the trees outside his window shaking and rolling against the heavy wind. He suddenly remembered that it was five years ago to the night that his father disappeared and he looked beyond the silver treetops at the full moon which had slipped low on the horizon and had an odd reddish tint. Strange, he thought, the moon resembled the glow-in-the-dark planet stickers above his bed; the ones he and his mom cut out and pasted on the wooden ceiling. He was still drowsy, and the moon appeared to him to be one of those stickers. Squinting through the trees he expected to see the man-in-the-moon, but satisfied that all was good Alexander laid back on the pillow. However the whistling wind made it impossible for him to go back to sleep. And he had a lot on his mind considering that tomorrow was his first day at a new school!

Alexander hated these nights! The old, creaky house made a symphony of noises -- squeaking, grinding and crunching -- that could drive *anyone* nuts.

No wonder old Ms. McCoy, the previous owner, had gone mad. She never slept. The house was haunted. Alexander was sure of that. Everyone in town said so too. He tried telling his mom, but she denied it.

The clock showed 11:09. "Ugh, almost midnight," he moaned into a yawn, and thought about the new school he was going to tomorrow. He wasn't happy about it but it wasn't his decision. Now that his mother was teaching at the school, all he heard was how "wonderful Forrestville was, and how lucky he was to go there for free." He loved learning and found his last school easy. Why did his mom have to mess things up? Perhaps, it's...

He didn't want to think about it now. He knew he'd be tired in the morning if he stayed up worrying. Maybe a glass of milk would help him get back to sleep, he thought. He got out of bed to go down to the kitchen.

The house was pitch black, but Alexander knew his way around now so he didn't even bother to turn on the lights. He opened his door, took three steps, and hopped over to the gnarled, wooden staircase. Down he went on the creaky stairs, avoiding the maze of bumps and nails sticking up like booby traps. The creaking could wake up the devil, but not his mom, who, as usual, had fallen asleep to the blaring TV in her room and couldn't hear a thing. He hopped off the last step, held on to the brass knob at the end of the banister and flung himself into the kitchen. He poured a glass of milk, warmed it up in the microwave and drank half of it in one gulp. He was still feeling anxious and was fully awake so he decided to go into the library.

The library was the only room Alexander really liked. He flicked the light switch, illuminating two massive metal chandeliers above his head, exposing the thousands of books on massive bookcases that lined the walls. When his dad sat in the room in his plush red chair by the fireplace the room seemed cozier, but since his dad's mysterious disappearance the library felt big and cold. His mom never lit the fire any more, except on holidays. She said it was too hard to care for. Alexander missed the fire. He missed chopping wood when his mom let him, but even without the fire, he was happy to sit in the library for hours.

And he did spend hours and hours alone in the library as he hadn't made any friends in the neighborhood. He didn't blame them. After all, he was the kid in the haunted house. But he didn't have much to do and the house didn't have cable or satellite TV. His computer was old too, so he couldn't play any of the cool games his classmates constantly talked about. He would have asked his mom for a new computer, but in spite of it being old he could make it do wonders, as if guided by supernatural forces. And his computer helped him do his homework, making him the smartest student in his school… until now!

Now, in this new house Alexander would come home from school, do his homework and wander into his father's library; this giant cavern with its bookcases reaching up to the rickety ceiling.

This library had books in just about every language. There were plays, novels, biographies, philosophy books… everything. Tiny books that were paper thin and big fat books with embroidered red and gold covers. Alexander would run his hands over the old books with their magnificent covers dating as far back as 1899, 1750, 1650. He had even found one dated 1550.

His dad had pointed this particular book out to him several times. It was a small leather-bound book with a carving of a beautiful cross on its cover. His dad had told him that it was very special. It was the second half of the Bible and was called the Stephanus Greek New Testament. Written in the original Greek language, it was one of the most important books ever printed. Most of the Bibles that followed, even the ones read today, were based on this version. His dad told Alexander that his greatest love was collecting rare books and he saved all his money to buy these. He said that this book especially, was worth a lot of money, and because it held so many secrets, he kept it hidden it in a safe to which only Alexander and his mom had the combination... But his mom didn't seem to care about books.

Oh, how he missed his dad! He was a military man; a Captain at Forrestville Military Training Camp for the Elite Forces, and a super smart soldier. He had disappeared during a secret military mission but his mother believed he was still alive. "Dad is too brilliant a soldier to vanish," his mom often told him. The military commander would not say anything more than that Captain Grigory King was "Missing in Action"!

His dad spoke many different languages and could read these books. Alexander felt close to him when he spent time in the library. He used to hate reading, though he had to hide this from his mom, but now the more he read the books in his dad's library, the more he became fascinated with books. He started at one end and decided that he could work his way to the other end by the time he was twenty years old. There were at least

1000 books there, so he would have to read at least 100 a year. That would be eight or nine every month!

He loved the science books the best, but although many were still too hard for him to really understand, he was managing. He had to look up many words, which annoyed him at first, but soon he saw it as a treasure hunt; he wanted to find and understand all these fascinating words. He came across words like 'fubsy,' which meant short and fat, so he started to call the mean kids in school 'fubsy'. He would make it sound like a compliment, so they didn't know he was making fun of them. He seemed to get away with it, except the one time when he called Devlin Ratner 'fubsy'. Devlin outsmarted him and had looked it up. Then during recess, he and his two goons, Christian Chung and Cain Cavoli, beat Alexander up. Devlin became Alexander's arch enemy and he too, was transferring to Forrestville. Enough, thought Alexander. He and Devlin hadn't had a fight for more than a year, but they still hated each other. As he drank the rest of his milk, he looked around the big library room. He would rather think about his dad.

The more time he spent in the library, the more he felt a kinship with the house. When he felt brave, he would explore its many secret rooms and passageways, and was always excited to find his way back to where he started from. The real estate agent had told them that this house was once an important stop on the Underground Railroad, which was a network of houses where courageous families hid slaves during their escape from slavery on their way to freedom. Alexander loved to explore all the nooks and crannies; all the secret compartments and passageways. It was a treasure trove, and he loved the fact that everyone in Forrestville believed his house to be haunted.

His classmates loved to creep around his house after school, and on Thursdays Devlin Ratner would bring a group of the nastier kids around who would brag about it at school the next day. Now, as he sat in the library, Alexander could hear their footsteps in the driveway or hear rustling through the trees. He'd hear the kids saying, "Watch out for old Ms. McCoy's ghost. If she sees you, she'll grab you and tear the skin right off of your face! She'll eat your eyeballs and fry your brain and feed it to her three-headed dog."

Alexander knew better. The ghost was not Ms. McCoy but that of her uncle William McCoy. The real story was told to him by Doug Berg, the old mailman.

During a gruesome fight over a woman with his brother Winston, William hit his head badly and he went mad. Winston locked him up in the annex right above Alexander's room and fed him like he was a dog. Eventually, William hanged himself and for some reason couldn't leave, and had been haunting the house ever since.

He wanted Devlin Ratner and his friends to believe the worst and be scared. He would wait for them to get close to the house and when he saw they were hiding under the dry bush, he would run upstairs to the second floor window, grab an old Halloween toy his father had brought back from Germany, and kneeling below the window so he couldn't be seen, he would press the little red button on the back of the toy, which let out a terrifying, high-pitched scream. The squirrels in the nearby trees would scatter away. Devlin's boys would hit the ground, fall flat on their faces and cover their ears. Alexander would then slam his window shut, run through the hallway to his mom's room, open the window and scream at the top of his lungs, "No! No! No! Don't do it Ms. McCoy, please! Please!! Don't!! You already ate some of my brain yesterday!! I won't have any left! No, don't!! Help! Help me! Help me!" He would then scream for a while and slam the window shut. Then, he'd wait a few minutes, still crouching under the window-sill, before he would dare to look out to see the little invaders run for their lives, screaming, terrified that Ms. McCoy was going to eat their brains too.

Alexander became known as that strange kid in the haunted house, but no one could account for the fact that Alexander was a top student even as his brain was being eaten and that by now he really shouldn't have any brain matter left.   He really enjoyed the mystery he had created. He loved that people thought he lived with ghosts.

And he really was living in a haunted house. *WHACK! WHACK!* The sound of the shutters upstairs brought him out of his daydream. He looked at the clock above the doorway and saw it was 11:41 pm. Time to get back to bed, he thought, but as he glanced around the room, his eyes fell upon an old torn book on the top shelf that seemed out of place.

He hadn't seen this book before, and if he didn't know better, it looked to him as if someone had placed it there recently. He grabbed the ladder that was leaning against the bookcase, slid it around to the shelf, and climbed up. He removed the book and climbed back down. He wasn't tired any more. He sat back into his dad's chair and slowly and carefully opened the book, worried that he might damage it.

It was leather covered, just like the 1550 Bible, but the cover was just a plain worn leather. The stitching was rough as if done by hand. Alexander lifted the heavy cover and examined the first page. It contained the same Greek lettering as the 1550 Bible, but this book looked even older. The paper felt different and very delicate. He was super careful, afraid that it might crumble. There were already holes here and there on the page, and the edges were ragged, but the words on the page were unmistakably Greek, or at least that's what he thought:

πολλὰ μὲν οὖν ὑμῶν καὶ μεγάλα ἔργα τῆς πόλεως τῇδε γεγραμμένα θαυμάζεται, πάντων μὴν ἓν ὑπερέχει μεγέθει καὶ ἀρετῇ· λέγει γὰρ τὰ γεγραμμένα ὅσην ἡ πόλις ὑμῶν ἔπαυσέν ποτε δύναμιν ὕβρει πορευομένην ἅμα ἐπὶ πᾶσαν Εὐρώπην καὶ Ἀσίαν, ἔξωθεν ὁρμηθεῖσαν ἐκ τοῦ Ἀτλαντικοῦ πελάγους.

Those were the only words on the first page. Very carefully he leafed through the pages. He knew he would have to translate it and was about to close the book when his eyes fell on the inside of the cover where he saw the following words scratched into the leather:

Do not damage these scrolls, my son. Within you will find secrets you never dreamed of. Secrets only you must know. Secrets you must use when you are ready and are given the sign. I love you very much and always will. Love, dad.

Alexander's hands shook. A cold numbing sensation struck his throat, a sensation he experienced every time he tried not to cry. Why had he never seen this book before! This book was given to him by his dad, but he hadn't seen it before! His dad had left him a note! Had it been there the whole time and he never saw it? There were so many thoughts jumbling through Alexander's head, there was no way he'd get back to sleep tonight.

He'd swear he hadn't seen this book before, so how did it get here? Did Uncle Jim put it there? Maybe. Could his father be sneaking around undercover so as not to be detected by his enemies? It didn't seem likely. What was all this talk of "secrets"? His head was whirling.

WHACK! the shutters again banged on the window frames. He looked at the clock above the doorway: 11:55 pm. Maybe he could get to sleep before the ghost came out tonight. He raced upstairs so quickly he forgot to turn the light off, so he went back down, jumping over the bumps and nails in the staircase like a ninja, turned the light off, and raced back up the stairs, creating such a ruckus it sounded like a hurricane had hit the house. He was sure his mom would wake up, so before he went back up to his room he checked on her. She was fast asleep. He went back to his room and placed the secret book under his pillow. He had to go back to sleep before the ghost came out and he had to get some rest because it was his first day at the new school tomorrow. But his mind was still racing.

Bang! Whack! The wind battered the house's shutters and whistled through the trees. He had forgotten to close the shutters so he got out of bed, opened the window and reached outside so he could close them and lock them shut. A thunderstorm had darkened the sky. A sharp streak of lightning would light it up and violent thunder would rattle everything. Alexander counted two seconds between the lightning and thunder and calculated that the storm was only 2 miles away. Rain was already pouring down as he closed the windows.

Alexander saw his reflection in the window. He wasn't fond of his look. His slightly elongated head was covered with a mop of wild curly brown hair; hair that looked like a jungle not a head of hair. Trying to straighten it with a comb would only make it curl back into a mop. He also wore oversized horn-rimmed glasses and was made fun of for this, and his hair, and for being short… which some kids attributed to the ghost eating away at his brain. But it wasn't just the kids; adults also looked at him in a weird way.

Once while the class was sitting for a class picture, the principal made a comment to the photographer, "Look at this one," he pointed at Alexander, "he looks like a monkey, with that mop of hair, doesn't he?" Alexander was embarrassed but there wasn't anything he could do. He just had to learn to live with it. Maybe life at Forrestville Academy would be different, but with Devlin Ratner being there too, it might not be.

CRACK! WHACK! The thunder, lightning, clanged around the house. He jumped back from the window. The house shook. The sound of the thunder reverberated through the hallways. Alexander clambered back into bed and grabbed one of the pillows, covering his head with it. All was quiet when a sudden loud click made him jump. He looked up as the grandfather clock showed 11:59. He had insisted since he was six years old that this clock be in his room, despite its noisy tick, tock. That was just before his dad disappeared. It was one minute to midnight.

"Damn," Alexander sighed. He hated being up at midnight. He slid his butt down and lay on his back. He wrapped his sheets around him and buried his face in the pillow, covering his ears too. He peeked out to watch the clock ticking away towards midnight. Thirty seconds to go. He wished he could take a team of Army Special Force soldiers up to the attic; maybe they would slow down the time. Ten seconds... nine... eight

maybe it wouldn't be so bad this time, maybe it wouldn't happen at all—six... five—maybe he would forget this time, he would ask—three... two... one...

BANG! BANG! BANG!

BANG! BANG! BANG!

"Don't guess," he whispered to himself and curled up in his sheets like a tortoise in its shell. The banging on the ceiling above his bed continued incessantly. Then came the footsteps... Someone was pacing back and forth. Why wasn't he used to it by now, he wondered? The moon still looked odd, but the wind had stopped. So did the whistling of the wind and the trembling of the trees. All he heard was the pacing... but he knew the screaming would begin soon.

"Help me!" came the whimpering. Then more loudly, "Help me! HELP ME!" There it was, right on time. It got louder and louder. "Untie me! I want out! LET ME OUT!!!! LET ME OUT!!! The screams got louder and louder and very frightening.

"Stop!" called out Alexander. It didn't stop.

Alexander took a deep breath and sighed as he pulled his cover over his head. He stayed that way for a while, wanting his dad more than ever at times like this. One day, he thought, he would let the ghost out, but first he had to figure out how to get up to the attic. He hadn't found the secret entrance yet. Maybe he was too scared to look by himself. Then the screams died away and he came out from under his covers, but the wind had begun to pick up again. He tried to think about something else and his thoughts turned to how he was going to scare Devlin Ratner. The next time Devlin Ratner and his crew came to the house he would have a surprise for them. His mood changed. It was better to think about how much fun it was to live in this house in spite of the weird goings-on. He wondered why his mom wasn't aware of it. Could it be that the noise from the TV drowned it all out?

The wind got louder. It was so loud that he didn't know if he would get any sleep this night. So he focused on how much he'd enjoy the kids talking about him and saying things like he was the scariest, weirdest, most terrifying kid they'd ever met. With those thoughts, and with a smile, he dozed off.

*   *   *

He slept more deeply than usual, and his recharged "computer brain" began the vivid dreams that he had every night. But tonight these dreams were clearer, more vivid and in truly magnificent colors. They were real and lucid. Chances are, he later thought, they were triggered by vibrations from the ancient book under his pillow.

In his dream, he is walking toward the mountains behind his house, and has gone much deeper into the wild than he had ever been. He keeps walking on the crooked narrow animal path surrounded by dense vegetation… grass, bushes, and trees. But he is still far from the end of the tree line; the point where trees can no longer grow. The trees surrounding him are still big and majestic and very lush. Suddenly there is a loud scream as a huge flock of frightened birds flies overhead racing to get out of the way, apparently from some danger. He has gone too far. He is in the wild and it is dangerous. A terrifying predator could attack at any moment. He bends down, grabs a big stick, cuts off its leaves with his pocketknife, then whittles it into a dagger. He then moves close to a big tree, ready to climb to safety if needed.

Expecting an attack any moment, Alexander snaps into full alert. He moves his eyes and his head from side to side like a radar screen, searching for signs. Suddenly a sound in the bushes in front of him draws his attention. He freezes. A moment later the head of a creature pops out of the bushes… A human-like head with pointy ears, no facial hair, a mop of brown curly hair not much different from his own, but with long locks all the way down its neck. He watches the creature moving towards him, its body like a lion or a Sphinx-like cat. White hair covers its body except for its huge claws. Its forelimbs have a cover of black making it look like it's wearing a tuxedo jacket, or maybe a military uniform.

The creature, this big cat, is now out of the bushes, stops and sits looking a little like the Egyptian Sphinx. He seems to be welcoming. Alexander notices that thickened skin folds on both shoulders appear to be wings. "It is a Sphinx, a real Sphinx," he confirms. He adores the Egyptian Sphinx and has dreamt about Giza and the pyramids. He was fascinated by how they protected the ancient Egyptian Pharaohs and their treasures. The ancients created mythical Sphinxes with human heads and mighty beast-like lion bodies to show that these guardian creatures were as smart as humans but strong like beasts. And they had wings to fly.

The Sphinx in front of him doesn't have wings and he concludes that whatever this creature is protecting doesn't require flight. But what or who is it protecting? It is just sitting there staring at him. It wasn't going to attack. It moves its head beckoning Alexander to follow. Alexander just stands there. Then he hears it make some sounds that sounded like, "C oo-m m - on ". "C oo-m m - on ". Then it stands up and begins to move forward on two front legs. Curious, he was always curious, so Alexander takes a few steps toward the creature, which turns and repeats, "C oo-m m - on "!

Alexander follows the Sphinx up the narrow forest trail overgrown with vegetation. He notes several narrow paths on the left leading into underground caves.

He wonders what is below in these underground caves. They could be mining tunnels filled with scary monsters or elaborate underground palaces with treasures of gold and gemstones.

After a while the vegetation thins and the landscape becomes rocky. The clouds lift and Alexander can see a bright moon peeking out through the treetops. The sky, crystal clear, covered with billions of twinkling stars, one constellation he had not seen before blinks like a road sign and is shaped like an arrow. It seems to be pointing to a spot on the path they were on. Is it a sign that he is welcomed and even expected?

There are no more wild sounds from scary monsters or frightened birds. It is as if the Sphinx creatures control this world. It is safe. He sees silhouettes of other human-lion like creatures, and at one twist on the path he sees another Sphinx behind a heavy bush. He feels that he is being protected. Like he is on a special mission. The scenery is mysterious but beautiful. The stars flicker like diamonds.

The path comes to a sharp turn to the right. For a few seconds, Alexander can't see the mythical creature but then sees it turn left into a narrow lane. The path appears to be ending at a huge boulder overgrown with wild plants. Alexander stops walking, worried that he has walked into a trap.

The mighty human-lion creature stops, puts its shoulder against the obstruction and pushes. His strength is not human. The boulder slowly moves and creates a gate-like opening that unveils a well-manicured lane leading into a well-lit tunnel. The human guard in a lion's body beckons Alexander by moving forward and calling "Let's go - C oo- m m- on". It enters the cave tunnel now, on four limbs. Alexander follows the mighty Sphinx creature.

The cave entrance is narrow and appears unremarkable, but soon it begins to widen as they move into the main tunnel. It is well lit, magnificently covered with marble and lined with shiny gemstones. It is a majestic entrance; nothing like anything Alexander has ever seen. The long entrance hall is lined with Sphinxes... human guards, each with a lion's body, sitting on their hind legs. They bow to Alexander as he passes. He feels like a warrior, a Chosen One, being honored after a victory.

The glorious entrance opens up into an awesome and impressive circular hall with majestic columns and statues surrounding this grandiose rotunda. There are four big human-lion guards protecting this entrance hall, all resting on marble columns. There is one at each side of the entrance to the glorious vestibule and two in front of a colossal and majestic golden doorway at the opposite side of the entrance. The doors are stained with gold and silver and have impressive carved figures as decoration.

The silence is suddenly broken by the sound of a large bronze Gong being struck by one of the Sphinx. Thirteen loud vibrating bell sounds are heard echoing through the corridors. The penetrating sound causes the mighty human-animal guards to focus their attention on the large golden door. Alexander finds himself in the middle of the hall and his Sphinx next to the engraved gold and silver door. Suddenly the door swings open, exposing a big low-lit capacious rotunda lined with colossal columns and statues and a massive circular marble staircase in the center hall, leading downstairs. The rotunda is lined with dark marble and golden columns. This grand vestibule is different from the grandiose entrance tunnels, and the gloriously lit rotunda hall. This room is impressive, but it reminds Alexander more of a funeral home than a palace.

His Sphinx now accompanied by two mighty human-lion guards begins descending the impressive staircase. Alexander follows them for at least three stories. There are two columns on each side of stairway and a hall leading toward another massive door. Two more giant human-lion creatures emerge and position themselves at each side of the door.

The door looks like the entrance to Fort Knox, where billions of the US gold bullion reserves are secured behind bullet-proof doors and guarded by well-armed soldiers. As he looks around his mind is spinning. What are these mighty guard creatures protecting? Is it a treasure vault with diamonds, jewels, gold coins? A God, an Egyptian Pharaoh, or the key to a Secret Code, a code that could help create a better world?

The first mighty lion creature makes a loud yell, "O--

ou- o u uu o," and is joined by the others. It sounds like a lion song and after a few minutes of this immense sound, the large door opens. Two very large human-like persons in head scarves and long gowns emerge, followed by several, similarly dressed male figures. The mighty human-lion guards stay outside and continue to guard the place. The chamber is lit up with enormous candles.

He hears his name called, "Alexander, come on into our sanctuary, my man," a deep voice roars.

Alexander enters slowly and notices a big glass box at the center of the room. The large humans lead him toward a glass covered throne. Sitting on it is a mystical human, his head bowed, his chin resting on his right fist. He resembles Rodin's 'The Thinker' sculpture. His right elbow rests comfortably on the arm of a majestic antique throne. The throne is made of gold and the wood, silver stained. The seat and arm rest are blue velvet. The majestic looking being holds a golden scepter in his left hand and seems to be in a trance.

The human guard pushes Alexander in front of the mighty being, as the other guards form a half circle around him. Standing straight, Alexander looks unafraid, and looking at him, and conjuring up all his meditative powers, he breathes deeply and tries to send mental messages and vibrations to break whatever trance this majestic being is in. He is perspiring profusely as he continues working all his powers. The powers he had learned from his dad.

The majestic being raises his head, sending a shock wave through the room and a loud "U-uu u u- h" from the Sphinx. He stands up, his lean body towering over everyone and everything in the room. He lifts his scepter with his right hand, and points it over Alexander's head. A blissful lightning charge is followed by a booming sound shattering the glass-like throne into thousands of pieces. The mystical being steps down and walks toward Alexander. His guards run to help him, as the chief guard yells in amazement, "Oh h-boo-n-never b-before".

The mystical being puts both hands on Alexander's shoulders, their eyes locked; their souls connected.

"My son," his voice booms, "You are the chosen one. You will lead us to power and peace."

Alexander stammers out "I do not under…" but the mystical being puts his fingers on Alexander's lips signaling him to be quiet.

Looking into Alexander's eyes, he says, "Ask no questions and never doubt your own strength. We will guide you. Have no fear." The guards bow, as he places the scepter on Alexander's head. With a flash of lightning, Alexander's head is illuminated with a crown. He is sworn in as the *New Prince*.

* * *

Outside the wind howled and thunder and lightning opened the sky. A powerful wind broke the window latch and Alexander jolted awake and back to this world. He could feel the scepter on his shoulder and the crown on his head. But when he touched his head, there was no crown. He went over what happened. The book, the trip into another world, and being crowned a prince who could save the world.

He got out of bed and fastened the metal latch on the window to stop the banging. The dream was real to him, and he jumped back into bed intending to go back to the mystical kingdom. He needed answers. He was so exhausted from the night's activities that he managed to fall back to sleep as soon as his head hit the pillow, falling into a deep dreamless sleep.

Forrestville Academy

WHACK! – WHACK!

The whole house echoed when Alexander's mother violently hit the banister with her broom. It was so loud that even the hallway lamp made a whistling sound. Throughout the house every sound reverberated like a cello. The walls in Alexander's room shook, but when he was dreaming powerful dreams that kept him in a deep-sleep state; he heard nothing that happened in the real world around him.

WHACK! - WHACK! -WHACK!

His mom was banging the banister harder now. Alexander poked his head out from under his blanket. "Oh no, not Mr. McCoy again," he whispered.

"Alexander did you leave the refrigerator door open?!!!" his mom yelled as he opened his eyes.

"Did you?!!!" she called again.

He stared at his headboard as the morning sun threw a strong bright light at the old wood board. The bed had belonged to the old gold miner Mr. McCoy who was the architect of this monster mansion. The wood was stained green and there was a painted carving in the center. Alexander loved the painting of the Naval Officer who stood at attention in front of a large military sailboat which was much like the ship in the painting of George Washington crossing the Delaware, but smaller. That painting hung on the wall of his history classroom, but Alexander's was much more interesting. On his

23

painting the Naval Officer was dressed in a blue jacket festooned with an assortment of gold stripes, medals, pins, and buttons. He wore bright white pants, black boots and a glitzy military cap on his head. One foot was resting on an anchor-post in front of the white sails and he held a large golden telescope close to his right eye. "Captain Harry Bluewater," read the inscription.

"Oh, what I would give to be Harry!" he thought to himself as he stared at his favorite Captain and he began to drift back to dreamland. He would have a fancy cap to cover the jungle of hair on his head. He would be an explorer. He would discover new oceans and lands and have people everywhere being nice and who would call him "Sir". Maybe one day he would be a great explorer and find islands with buried treasures; perhaps even find where his dad was being held and rescue him. He would load his new treasures on to his boat and sail back home with his father.

"Are you awake?!!!" his mom yelled again, her voice penetrating deep into his room.

Alexander tumbled out of bed, stumbled to the door, opened it, and yelled back. "I don't remember!!!" The house didn't have an intercom system, but it was big enough to need one. His Mother was becoming more and more paranoid about the possibility that someone would break into the house. Her brother, Jim Rey, was a traveling salesman for a large corporation, and would pass through the town and leave her a note that he was there. Jim knew she was always expecting a sign that his dad was back from his secret mission.

Mary King, Alexander's mom, started her day at 5:45 am, and expected Alexander to wake up soon after so they could have breakfast together. Alexander loved spending time with his mother and leaving for school made him sad. She was the only person in his life who cared if he was even alive.

Today appeared to be like any other school day, but it was very different. He was starting a new school. He finished his cereal and started to get nervous. What would Forrestville Academy be like? He wished he didn't have to change schools as he obviously had little in common with the wealthy and privileged kids there. They may be as smart or even smarter than him, and most of them were boarders who lived at the school. He would be different even there. He actually lived in the town. And to top it off, his arch enemy Devlin Ratner was going to be there too! Did his mom *want him* to be miserable for the next six years?

"Go get your backpack, and make sure you have your schedule. Oh, it's going to be so exciting Alexander! Aren't you excited?" said his mom lovingly.

"Nah... I guess," he replied, though his face clearly showed he didn't believe it.

"Oh! cheer up. You're going to make many new friends. It'll be better than last year. You'll have kids in your class who are just as smart as you and they'll be interested in the same books! It'll be fun."

"Yeah, I know," he said sheepishly.

"Go get your stuff," she said reassuringly. Alexander got up and was starting up the stairs when his mom called after him, "Oh, and bring down your tie so I can tie it for you! I'll meet you in the car. Don't forget your blazer! I sewed the Forrestville seal on for you last night!"

"Yeah, *okay*!" Alexander said, trudging up the stairs. His feet disappeared at the top of the staircase. Mary stared at the empty stairs. "It's a shame your dad couldn't teach you," she thought, her eyes tearing over. Alexander trudged to his room, snatched the schedule off his desk and shoved it into his backpack. He grabbed the ancient book from under his pillow, looked at it, kissed it and hid it behind some other book on the bookcase. He took another look at his headboard. Maybe he could consider today to be like the sea was for Captain Harry Bluewater; exploring a new place, dealing with the unknown, and becoming stronger and able to deal with new experiences and not be scared. Because going to a new school was very scary!

He shrugged off the earlier daydream, turned around and grabbed the red tie off the hook from inside his closet door, zipped up his backpack and went back downstairs. He ran outside and slammed the door behind him. He hopped into the passenger seat of his mom's car, which his mom had already started, and after an awkward lesson on tying his tie, they drove out of the driveway into the long winding roads that led from the castle to the school.

*   *   *

About twenty minutes later, Harkens Tower—the pride of Forrestville Academy—could be seen sprouting above the trees that surrounded and speckled the school's campus. From far away the buildings were a collection of magnificent stone forts. Alexander had seen the tower before, but he had not been close to the Academy. They drove further and further along the road, with trees on the left and the school's spear-like black fence on the right, until they reached the Forrestville gates. The fence ran right into two miniature stone towers, to which two giant black gates were pinned. That fence was so massive it looked like it could hold a dragon. The gates were open revealing a long driveway lined with enormous trees that shot up into the sky. Never had he seen trees as big and old as these were. There must have been at least thirty and each had to be at least a hundred or a hundred-and-fifty feet high. They lined both sides of the driveway in absolutely perfect formation. In fact it looked too perfect. Alexander hunched over in his car seat and tilted his head up so he could see the tops of the trees. Ahead he could see the end of the driveway and an opening leading into the thick base of Harkens Tower.

"Wow!" Alexander exclaimed. He had been terrified of his first day but now became more relaxed. He sat back in his seat, looked ahead at the school and forward to his first day.

"I told you you'd like it. Are you more excited now?"

his mom asked with an understanding smile. She understood that children are afraid of change, but adventures excite them, and they usually forget what worried them.

"Yeah," he said. He was now completely absorbed in the world he saw from the car window. It really was an amazing place. But although not wanting to admit it, it was still a little scary.

The car whizzed past the trees and came to a stop at the foot of the gigantic tower. There were several people in orange vests directing parents where to park and children to their classes. "Now get out sweetie and go to that building over there," his mom said, pointing to a red brick building with white trim on the windows. The entrance was a huge tower that seemed stuck in the middle of the small building's face. Did they really need to put a tower on *every* building, thought Alexander? "Ask for Mrs. Andrews' room," his mom continued, "She's expecting you. I have to run to teach my first class. I'll probably have to stay a little later to talk to some of the teachers, so you just come back to this spot and take the school bus. Okay?"

"Okay," replied Alexander.

"You can ask one of the security guards which bus you should take. Okay."

"Okay," he said again, sadly.

"You're going to have a great time, sweetie. I love you." He hated when she babied him and called him sweetie! "I love you too," he whispered, hoping that no one would hear him. He got out of the car, came around to the driver's side, kissed his mom goodbye and watched her drive into the parking lot.

Now he was on his own. He straightened his blazer and adjusted its shoulders for more comfort. He would never get used to wearing it, he thought. He turned and looked up at the building across the giant lawn, thinking… I really hope Mrs. Andrews knows who I am.

"Yes, that's the way," called the security guard, noticing the nervous and bewildered Alexander. Alexander looked up for a moment. Oh, he *was* talking to me…

"Oh, okay. Thanks!" Alexander replied, slightly embarrassed. He started to walk and fell in with one of the many groups zipping by him. They seemed to know where they were going! He blended into the group that seemed to be heading in the same direction. The guide seemed to be giving a talk to the group and he listened attentively and learned about the school's history. The guide was saying, "This is the oldest school in the West and was founded by a clergyman named William Marshall Harkens. He moved West in 1848 during the gold rush. He became the first ranch owner and became very successful. He wanted to do something for the town and decided to start its first school, becoming its first teacher. There were only twenty pupils in a little shack by the river. Today, there are two hundred middle-school and four hundred high-school students, and it has become one of the premier private high schools in the country! Twenty-five percent of our graduates have gone to Harvard, Yale, and Princeton," the guide exclaimed, and proudly added, "Its endowment has ballooned from five hundred dollars in 1867 to two billion today!"

Alexander wasn't quite sure what all of that meant, but he was impressed and enjoyed listening. He wondered if any of this should matter to him although he couldn't see how. The group suddenly stopped. They had come to his building! Alexander left the group and scurried up the stone stairs. He found the lobby and shouted a big "WOW!" - as if things couldn't get any more extravagant! The lobby wasn't especially big, but Alexander's eyes looked at the floor and followed the grey veins that curved their way through the cream-colored marble. The veins looked kind of like the roads that led to his house! He looked over the furniture— wooden chairs, benches, and little coffee tables covered with magazines - painted gold and black. The bottom four feet of the walls was plated with three-inch thick black marble. The top half of the walls was a basic white, and covered with huge portraits of very important, and really *old*-looking men and women. The largest picture hung in the center and at the end of the main corridor was a portrait of a very powerful looking gentleman. He looked very impressive, with a large forehead and a full head of wild hair. He resembled President Andrew Jackson but was even more impressive. He had on grey pants, a white shirt, and a bright red vest, finished off with a long grey coat that fell to his knees, and black shoes.

Alexander was impressed with the vest and the bright white shirt under it. The shirt was tied at the collar by something that resembled a bow-tie, but not quite... Whatever it was, it was elegantly wrapped around the man's broad neck and gave him an authoritative look. Alexander's eyes focused on the gold engraved letters on a large plate below the frame:

William Marshall Harkens

Founder of Forrestville Academy

So that was Harkens. He was impressive. His eyes then fell on the placard to the right of the portrait.

SIR S. F. MOORE

1832 – 1914

William Marshall Harkens

Oil Painting on Canvas

Looking back at the Harkens portrait, Alexander stared in awe at the fiery look in his eyes. The artist really captured him. He must have been even more fiery a hundred years ago.

Someone bumped into him and knocked him off his feet.

"Oh my God, I'm *sooo* sorry," said a very tall older girl. "I didn't even see you there, I'm *really*, really sorry. Let me help you up."

"Yeah, thanks," Alexander said, slightly embarrassed that he got knocked over by a girl. She helped him up and continued walking with another girl who was giggling. Probably at him, thought Alexander.

"Sorry. See you later!" the tall girl said, looking back.

"Yeah, see you later," said Alexander dusting himself off and checking his belongings. As the two girls walked away, he overheard the tall girl comment to her friend, "Oh my god, he's so short I didn't see him!" They both giggled. Alexander knew they weren't being mean, but it hurt. He looked again at Harkens' portrait and as he stared back at him, he glanced away for a moment, then glanced back as the portrait winked at him. He jumped! Whooo!!!!! What just happened, he thought. No, he thought, he must have blinked. He narrowed his eyes and moved closer to examine the painting. The eyes were unchanged, so Alexander decided that he had winked, not the portrait. It made sense. But something was different. His mouth looked different too. It seemed to turn upward, giving him a slight smirk. He hadn't noticed that before.

"Some picture, huh?" an older woman commented as she passed by. Alexander spun around and looked up at her. She smiled and he smiled back.

"Yeah. Some picture," he replied. Then he saw it again out of corner of his eye. The picture winked again. NO WAY, he thought. It was creepy. He was stunned. Could Harkens look out for him? He was, after all, the school's founder.

But that was a crazy idea Alexander decided. He

looked in the direction the woman had gone and saw an ornate clock above the front door he had entered. He saw that if he didn't hurry he would be late. He saw the REGISTRATION → sign on a stand next to the table with a big bouquet of flowers on it. He was relieved and looking back at the painting he winked at it.

It may be crazy, but Alexander felt a little better now, not at all nervous. The painting made him feel like he was going to be all right. He turned around and followed the sign which was pointing towards an office with several pleasant older ladies sitting at individual desks. One of them turned out to be the nice lady who spoke to him in front of the painting. He met Mrs. Andrews who gave him his locker number and combination, and a map that would help him find the different buildings that his classes were in. That was new for him. His classes were held in any of the three buildings, which were not necessarily close to each other.

"Don't worry about it, Mr. King. You'll get used to it and you'll be fine," Mrs. Andrews said reassuringly. "Let's have a look at your schedule."

"Oh, right," said Alexander and pulled his crumpled schedule out of this backpack. He put down his backpack and tried to flatten out the paper before handing it to Mrs. Andrews, who just waited and smiled. "Don't worry about it. Okay, so your first class is Professor Finley's class 'Origins of the Universe'. I know that sounds scary, but it's really just science, which I've heard you're *very* good at."

"Yeah, I like it a lot," said Alexander a little embarrassed, "I know it's kind of nerdy."

"It's nothing of the sort! Everyone here is a little nerdy, so you'll feel *right* at home soon enough. Okay, so this class is in Albert Hall. Check your map and follow the signs in the left corner. Do you see it?"

"Yeah, I see it."

"Okay, so trot along now and get there. You want to get there early so you can get a good seat. When the bell rings, all the students are going to rush in, so get there soon, okay?"

"Sure," said Alexander, happy to have talked to the pleasant Mrs. Andrews. Forrestville Academy isn't all that bad if everyone is as nice as she was, he thought.

As Alexander left the registration building, he strolled along the asphalt pathways that criss-crossed an endless number of beautifully groomed green patches of grass, some even dotted with red, yellow, and purple lilies. He finally came to another, very similar-looking, red brick building with the words "ALBERT HALL" hanging on a huge metal plaque above the giant archway that led into the building. Alexander walked up the stone stairs. It took him some time to find the classroom, hoping to get a good seat by the window away from the other kids. When he found the room, there were so many kids there already he worried that he wouldn't even find a seat. He looked around looking lost.

"Are you new?" said a very pretty older girl with a

gentle smile.

"Umm, yeah," mumbled Alexander, so nervous he started to fidget with his hands and thrust them into his pockets. "I'm looking for Mr. Finley's class."

"Well you're in the right place," she said. Then she leaned in. Alexander's heart was racing. "But make sure to call him *Professor* Finley, okay? He won't forgive you if you don't." She winked at him. "Have a good time!"

"Thanks! You too!" he said after she had already turned around. What an idiot, he thought... 'you too?' who *says* that? Shaking his head, he headed for the door toward the crowd. When the bell rang out from the church steeple it echoed down the halls. In a split second, all the noise stopped and one of the kids flung open the door. Then the stampede began. As all the kids rushed in and scrambled for a seat, two huge jocks thought it would be funny to block them. They blocked the entrance and the crowd of kids were stuck in a giant traffic jam. "You don't want to make Finley mad guys! Come on, go inside!!" one of them shouted sarcastically. "Come on, what you are waiting for?" asked the other, like he didn't know why.

"You know what he'll do to you Evan," said a girl's voice.

"Eh, whatever. I'm bigger than he is now," Evan scoffed, as he pushed a poor student in the face with his backpack.

"Come on Lim! Why don't you pay me for a good

seat, and I'll make sure you get it," the bully said to a small Asian boy with thick glasses.

"Shut up," Lim replied. "Leave me alone and go fail a class. I hope you drown this season."

"Ha! Not me! I'm gonna be the best rower in the west, little man!"

Everyone was pushing forward, but the jocks were just too strong. But Alexander, despite his small size was determined to get to his seat. The last thing he wanted was to have to sit next to monsters like these two boys. So, glancing around he pushed next to one of the jocks, removed his backpack and ducked down on all fours. He crawled through Evan's legs pushing the bag in front of him and scurried to a desk at the front next to the window.

"Whoa, we got a little mouse! I haven't seen him before; he must be a *new* little mouse! Want some cheese little mouse?!" yelled Evan. He ended his blockage of the door and at least ten students fell over each other. Evan went to sit at the back of the room and was still laughing at Alexander, making fun of his hair and glasses. It bothered Alexander but he ignored him. The kids here seemed to be as mean as they were in the public school. He expected better here in these fancy buildings. The kids found desks and chatted among themselves, sharing their summer holiday experiences. The girls hugged and the boys gave macho high fives and fisted handshakes. Some noticed the new kid and pointed at him.

BANG! The door flew open. BANG! BOOM! Bashing into the wall. The banging grew loud and the kids jumped. Apparently, Professor Finley entered by kicking the door open and startling the students. The door was about to hit the Professor in the face, but he caught the doorknob with his left hand and stopped it, grinning. "UP!" he roared. The students shot up like champagne bottle corks popping and stood at frozen attention next to their desks. Professor Finley was satisfied and slammed the door behind him. He glared at each student, sizing each up.

Professor James Finley was definitely the most distinguished character on campus. He had a thick Irish brogue that was immediately recognizable. Even if you couldn't see him you could hear him coming. He was always yelling at someone to tuck in their shirt or retie their tie properly. You had to make sure you were spic-and-span when you were around him. He was different. He had a limp, paralyzed right arm, but he kept a good posture and the stature of an English king. Some said he looked a lot like King Richard III, who had lived and died in the 1400s. During his reign he locked two young nephews in the Tower of London and killed them, making him the next in line to become king. The older Forrestville students had read Shakespeare's play and would joke that Professor Finley was the old king come back to life.

"Richard the Third didn't die," they whispered and spooked the younger kids, "he just changed his name to

Professor James Finley... ha ha." Others said Richard
did die but came back as a zombie called Finley.

Whatever the story, the kids feared him for a lot more
than because he looked like King Richard. He didn't
smile often and when he did, it was forced and seemed
to be hiding something hateful... maybe a hateful heart.
Yes, it was true. He demanded to be addressed
"Professor," not "Mr." or "Dr." He once taught
advanced quantum mechanics and astrophysics at
Oxford University in England. Being called "Professor"
made him swell with pride. He didn't hide his withered
arm but displayed it with pride; a symbol of superiority!

The students nicknamed him "The Whip," because
he used his paralyzed right arm as a whip. The
fingernails on his withered hand were long and sharp,
and he used it with precision to nick an offender's ear
and cause severe pain. If he felt particularly sadistic, he
would draw blood. And he was often sadistic. But like
so much at Forrestville the legend behind his paralyzed
arm remained shrouded in mystery.

Professor Finley glared at the student in the last row,
threw down his briefcase and grabbed a piece of chalk
from the blackboard. He was all business all the time.
Still turned towards the blackboard, he barked "Evan
tuck in your shirt, you vagabond!" Alexander turned
around and sure enough Evan was frantically stuffing
his shirt into his pants.

Professor Finley turned slowly and faced the
students.

"Before we begin, I want everyone to say hi to some of our new students, Devlin Ratner, Simon Nicholas, and Alexander King." Professor Finley pointed at each of them with a long piece of white chalk as he said each of their names. He looked back at Devlin. "Mr. Ratner, how is your father?"

"Oh, very good, sir," replied Devlin eagerly.

"I haven't seen him for too long. You must give him my best," Finley said in an oddly warm tone, strange to see this personal side of him.

Then he looked at Alexander. He stared at him for what seemed an eternity. "You are very welcome here Mr. King." Alexander didn't know what to say or why he was singled out. He hoped Finley couldn't smell his fear.

"Th-th-thank you *Professor* Finley," stuttered Alexander. The class laughed. Professor Finley shot the class a look and became quiet. He then turned back to Alexander, and welling with pride he exhaled, "I hope you get used to our school quickly. Our workload is much heavier than you're used to. Get ready for some serious work. Everyone say hello to Mr. King and help him get comfortable here." He paused, and with an awkward smile, he lifted his head and exclaimed, "Now to the lesson!"

"W-w-w-w-w-w-elcome," whispered Devlin Ratner from across the room, imitating Alexander's stuttering to the amusement of the students within earshot. Alexander glared at him. Devlin smiled back. Alexander was right; things here will be terrible because of Devlin Ratner.

Standing at the blackboard, Professor Finley wrote furiously, outlining the lesson plan for the day. He had fifty minutes to give his favorite lecture to his new class. The chalk screeched and sent chills up the spines of his students. He seemed to have mastered the sound and weaponized it in the classroom. The students' groans only increased his efforts. He put his left hand on the metal frame of the blackboard and bellowed in his thick Irish brogue, "Today we'll discuss the formation of the elements!" The class groaned, which made Finley, scrape the chalk against the metal frame so hard that the students tensed and covered their ears. "Put your hands on your *desks*!" Professor Finley bellowed as he began his lecture.

"Thirteen point seven billion years ago, the universe was nothing but a point. In fact, it was an infinitely small, infinitely hot, and infinitely heavy point." He paused. "What is the heaviest metal you can think of?"

"Iron?" called out a student from the back of the room.

"No!" Professor Finley growled, "Anyone else?"

"Lead?" said a pretty girl in the front.

"No, Ms. Harkens. In fact, lead will *float* on *mercury*."

Alexander's head shot up. Harkens? He wondered if she was related to his new friend in the painting. He'd have to look into it.

"Mercury," continued Professor Finley, "the liquid in a common thermometer is heavier than iron, copper, silver, and even lead." Professor Finley always exaggerated. It sounded like he was telling ghost stories at a campfire. "No one here could lift it. Not even you Jake." He pointed to a large kid in the middle row.

"Sure I could lift it," Jake replied, though he wasn't sure what Finley was talking about.

"Oh really?" asked Professor Finley with sadistic tone. "Go and pick up that basketball at the back." When Jake tried to pick it up, he found it very heavy and it tumbled out of his hands and rolled away as soon as he picked it up. The class exploded in laughter.

"Why is it so heavy?" Jake asked, shamefacedly.

Professor Finley squinted and barked, "It's filled with mercury, Jake. The same liquid metal that's in the thermometer your mommy uses when you're *sick*." "It's denser than steel, which means that if you filled that ball with steel it would be lighter than it is now. The only thing heavier is gold. If you changed an orange juice carton to pure gold, it would weigh 80 pounds!"

"Whoa," the kids reacted in unison.

"Oh, and a word of advice. Don't be stupid and try to drink the mercury in your thermometer. You'd lose all your hair, teeth, and nails. Get it Jake?... Sit down."

Professor Finley screeched his chalk again against the blackboard, silencing the class.

Satisfied, he moved on. "Now use your *imagination*. Imagine that the basketball is so dense, so full of heavy matter, that if you dropped it, it would go right through the floor, through the ground, and through the Earth. That would be something, wouldn't it? *But!* If it really was that heavy, it wouldn't move at all. Why?" He paused and waited for an answer. "Mr. *King*, what does something that heavy have?"

Alexander was terrified. "Uh… gravity?"

"Yes, gravity. What would something that heavy do if it had that much gravity? Would it fall through the earth?"

"No, it would make everything else move," Alexander said. Professor Finley continued to glare but there was a glimmer of surprise in his eyes.

"That's right, Mr. King. Well done. In fact, if that basketball was the beginning of the universe, it would be so heavy that its gravitational pull would suck the entire earth inside it. Could you imagine the entire earth fitting inside that basketball? It would suck *everything* inside it. Even you Jake. It would pull you toward its center and stretch you out like a piece of gum… forever and ever."

"Whoa!" the students exclaimed. "That's awesome!"

"Yes, it is." Professor Finley gave one of his wicked smiles. He was probably picturing what his students would look like stretched out like a piece of gum. "Well that was all there was…"

"What was around it?" asked a girl at the front of the room.

"Ha! That's just it... nothing," said Finley.

"You mean like empty space—"

"No!" he cut her off. "I mean like... *nothing*... that's the point. No one knows what *nothing* really is. No one knows what happens if you could reach the end of space; what's beyond it. Maybe one of you will become a scientist when you're older and make some great discoveries." Some kids at the back of the class snorted with laughter.

Professor Finley smirked. "Well I didn't *mean* you two back there. You won't likely do anything productive and will pump gas or live off your parent's money." Alexander couldn't believe a teacher would talk like that to his students. There was silence and shock around the room.

Professor Finley turned back to the board and the screeching sound continued. The chalk frequently made those awful, bone-chilling screeches against the hard, black surface, and with his left hand, drew ever-widening circles with great force, to illustrate the planetary orbits. His other arm just flailed about and followed the circular motion of his entire body. He appeared to fancy himself the Creator as he got more and more into his drawings, which were becoming very impressive.

He started to explain how that tiny point of infinity suddenly blew up, got bigger and bigger and bigger like a huge balloon with trillions and gazillions of microscopic grains of sand floating around inside. He asked them to imagine this balloon getting bigger and bigger until it exploded in a humungous **BIG BANG,** spreading out in a big circle. It continued to expand, like the way bread rises in the oven. As it expanded, it took all the particles with it as it widened.

As he talked, he seemed to become more and more agitated, waving his arms frantically, and his partially paralyzed right arm flailed like a string of link-sausages. With his left hand, he pressed the chalk to the board harder, more violently, and when he finished writing the words **BIG BANG** in big, bold letters, the chalk flew out of his hand and hit the board with such force that it splintered into a gazillion little pieces and seemed to explode into his face, sprinkling his hair with bits of chalky dust. Some of the chalk flew all the way across the room.

It was so violent, the students gasped. A few of the larger boys in the back, including Evan snickered, thinking that Professor Finley had really messed up this time. The rest of the class remained silent. Professor Finley turned sharply and faced them.

"What just happened here!?" he shouted, as if they were the ones responsible for the chalk explosion. They were puzzled; a few even sank back into their chairs. "Well!?" he said. "We just had a *big bang*, didn't we? The chalk, like one of the known Forces of Nature, contained particles that were positively or negatively charged. As the big bubble of our universe continued to expand, those positive and negative charges continued

to grow stronger and stronger, the particles grew bigger and bigger as they accumulated more and more cosmic dust and energy, until all of a sudden, we had... what? A critical mass? A huge, ever-widening black hole? A gigantic galloping gob of gaseous goop that could no longer contain itself! Well... can any of YOU explain it? No? Is this how the **BIG BANG** happened?"

The classroom was dead silent. The students stared up at Professor Finley in disbelief. If they moved their eyes from his heavily breathing body or his gnarled tree-trunk of a face, it was only to look behind him at the amazing diagrams on the blackboard, the pieces of chalk around the room, or the huge white mark Professor Finley had made on the blackboard.

The bell sounded, but the students remained in their seats, transfixed, immobile, and stunned by the realization that they had so much to learn. They got an important lesson today, and that was: Professor Finley was a great teacher.

The students eventually filed out of the room. Alexander was excited to go to his next class, though he knew it probably wouldn't be as exciting as Professor Finley's. This was like nothing he had ever experienced. It was amazing that as weird and as mean as Professor Finley was to his students, his made learning exciting. Alexander checked his schedule. His next class was in the same building but down one flight, in the basement. He headed up the stairs but as he got to the top he felt a sharp jolting push in his lower back. He tumbled halfway down the stairs before smashing into two older girls who held on to each other to keep their balance. Alexander fell the rest of the way like an awkward tumbling Slinky until he hit the wall at the foot of the stairs. He got up, very shaken, and tried apologizing to the two girls.

"Oh my god, I'm so, so sorry. I really didn't..."

"What the hell is your problem, freak? Think that's funny? Maybe you shouldn't try to grab girls on the stairway, and they'd talk to you more!" yelled one of the girls.

"No really, I really didn't do it. I..." Alexander looked up at the head of the stairs and saw Devlin Ratner trying to hide in a crowd that had gathered and was laughing. The others just stared at Alexander.

"You *did* do it, you little runt," said the other girl, who looked like she meant business. She literally towered over tiny Alexander like a colossus.

"No, he didn't!" came a voice from the crowd. Alexander looked up to see who was defending him. A pretty girl slightly taller than Alexander pushed her way through the crowd and walked down the stairs.

"He got pushed. It wasn't his fault. I saw the whole thing. It was another boy who pushed him from behind." Alexander knew it had been Devlin. He looked for him in the crowd but he was gone.

"I saw it as well," another student spoke up, "he was pushed in the back by some scumbag, who then ran away, Simon Nicholas, the new student, called out.

Alexander looked back at the girls apologetically.

"I'm really, *really* sorry," said Alexander. "I'm pretty banged up too. I fell all the way down the stairs," apologizing and also trying to gain a bit of sympathy.

The crowd started to disperse, having lost interest in the rather boring exchange of apologies.

"That's okay, I'm sorry I accused you," one of the girls said and handed him his backpack, which he hadn't noticed was lost as he tumbled down the stairs.

"Thanks," he said. As the girls began to walk away, Alexander turned to the girl who defended him. It was Ms. Harkens from Professor Finley's class! He was so distracted by all the commotion he didn't notice who it was.

"Thanks a lot. Devlin Ratner came from my old school. He hates me. I really didn't even want to come here 'cause I knew he was coming," he explained.

"He seems awful. Well, don't worry about it. There are a lot of nice kids here." She smiled and extended her hand. "I'm Rebekah."

"Hi, I'm Alexander. You can call me Alex, if you want." He smiled sheepishly.

"Nice to meet you, Alexander."

Alexander was a bit mesmerized. She was very pretty. He opened his mouth as if to say something but decided not to.

"What?" she said.

"Oh… umm… nothing, don't worry about it," said Alexander as he tried to backtrack.

"You can't do that. Now you have to tell me," she said.

"Well, okay. Professor Finley called you Ms. *Harkens*. Are you related to the Harkens who founded Forrestville?"

"Yes," she said, somewhat embarrassed, "he was my great, great, great grandfather. It's not that big of a deal."

"Wow, I think that's cool. I saw his picture in the main hall." He wasn't going to tell her that her great, great, great grandfather winked at him.

"Thanks," she said with a slight laugh. "Anyway, I've got to get to my next class, but it was nice meeting you. I hope you're not hurt. There's a nurse in Porter Hall if you think you should see her."

"No, I'm *great*!" Alexander said a bit too enthusiastically.

"Ha-ha. Okay," Rebekah said with a slight laugh. "see you around." And with that she went up the stairs.

"Yeah, see you around," he replied. He watched her for a few seconds then turned to go to his next class. Did he play that right? He always felt so awkward around girls! Well, he knew he had many changes to undertake to make a good impression in the future.

*   *   *

The rest of Alexander's classes were hardly eventful. He had basic math, which was really boring, history, and English. History was going to be interesting; they were going to study ancient Greece and Rome. The teacher, Mr. Henebry, a tall, burly man with a large black beard and flowing black hair, emphasized how relevant both civilizations were today. He was fascinated by Greece's strange inventions, like the "ship-shaker" that Archimedes invented to destroy large ships which was a huge claw that came from underneath the water, or like the Roman ballista, a gigantic crossbow that could shoot metal bolts over a thousand feet that would go right through a soldier's helmet! Alexander was also interested and excited about this class. Students at Forrestville were required to study both Latin and Greek, so he was especially excited to study the civilizations whose languages he would be learning. It wouldn't be as boring, he thought, if he could learn about these historic lands and their people. He had seen the movie "*300*" in spite his mom's protests, and liked it a lot.

He immediately liked Professor Henebry and enjoyed talking to him. Over the weeks he felt so comfortable with him that he asked him to translate the first page of his dad's secret book, which he still hid in the bookcase.

The professor said that the ancient message in the book came from Plato's *The Republic*, another book that was in his dad's library, and that he had read Plato's views on democracy a few times. The first paragraph his teacher translated was:

"Many, in truth, and great are the achievements of

your State, which are a marvel to men as they are here recorded; but there is one which stands out above all both for magnitude and for nobleness. For it is related in our records how once upon a time your State stayed the course of a mighty host, which, starting from a distant point in the Atlantic Ocean was insolently advancing to attack the whole of Europe, and Asia to boot. For the ocean there was at that time navigable."

Professor Henebry felt goosebumps when he read it, and explained that this section described an ancient state, perhaps Atlantis, and predicted the birth of a new empire one day; an empire that would unite the entire world into a noble republic, a democracy where we would all live together in peace, harmony, equality and happiness.

*　　*　　*

Next, he went to his English class and was surprised that his mom was the teacher. He was annoyed that he had to pretend she wasn't his mom, but so far school was great, and he knew he would enjoy all his classes.

The school had a fully diverse and integrated curriculum. History and literature were woven together to help the students understand the real world. You didn't come to this school to be coddled; you came to really learn, and Forrestville prided itself at challenging its students and providing them with the foundation to live a life of learning.

He didn't know what to make of this strange school,

but the day continued to be exciting. He knew that it would take him time to fully adjust, but he was prepared to like it there. The bell rang at the end of the day and Alexander walked over to his mom's office. She had just finished chatting with an older student, but when she saw him through the window, she signaled for him to wait.

His mom was very professional and didn't seem like his mom. It was great that she had this job and he was able to attend the school for free. It was a good opportunity for them both. He was glad that things worked out for them, but he missed his dad. If his dad would come home, his mom could be just his mom again.

When the student left and Alexander was able to go into his mom's office, she was happy to see him and apologized for keeping him waiting. "Here I'm a teacher first and your mom second. At least until the day ends." He smiled at her. He understood. "How were your classes today? How was Professor Finley's class?"

"It was scary, but really cool. I think he's crazy," replied Alexander. He hopped up on a desk with his feet dangling.

"Yes, I heard that. Well that's good. How were your other classes? History?"

"I liked history a lot. We learned about the cool inventions of the ancient Greeks and Romans."

"Wow that sounds fascinating. I'm so glad you had a good first day," his mom said. "We'll talk more at dinner tonight. I have to go to a short faculty meeting, so I'll walk you to the bus stop and see you at home, okay?"

"Okay," said Alexander, a bit disappointed.

"I promise I won't be long, okay?"

"Yeah, okay," he said and forced a smile.

They walked through the campus. It was his first day and he was feeling happy being there. A lot of the students had been there for years and their parents and grandparents and great-grandparents had gone there too. The school was an equalizer. No one was more important, no matter their family history. He had a feeling that he could do great things, especially with William Marshall Harkens looking out for him...

His mom kissed his forehead, hugged him and watched him get on the bus.

"I love you very much sweetie. I'm really proud of you. I'm glad you had a great day and want to hear all about it when I get home, okay?"

"Okay. Thanks mom," Alexander said with a smile. He preferred his mom to be a mom, and not his teacher. "Love you," she called after him.

"Me too," he called out as he got on the bus. He waded through the sea of kids and backpacks. The kids were turned around, kneeling on the seat and chatting. A few looked up at him, but most were busy chatting. He felt a push from behind and fell, face first, on the floor.

The floor of the bus was disgusting, with a mix of sticky strawberry milk and wet dirt, and it covered a side of Alexander's face. Someone was standing on his back as he struggled to get up. A piece of dirty green gum was pushing up against his eyelid, but he couldn't remove it because his arms were pinned down.

"I wuv you my wittle baaaaby…" said a squeaky voice. Devlin Ratner was imitating Alexander's mom.

"Get off me!" yelled Alexander.

"Oh the wittle baby wants to get up?"

"Get off!!" Alexander screamed.

"Whoa! Okay, dude, chill out. You're such a spaz," said Devlin. "No wonder your dad left you and your mom. He probably killed himself just to get away from you. Or he has a whole new family somewhere that he loves more."

Alexander pushed him off, spun around and hit Devlin so hard that his head banged against a seat and left him stunned. Devlin recovered and punched back.

The kids on the started to chant, "Fight! Fight! Fight!" until the Bus Driver stopped the bus, got up and pulled the two apart. He asked for their names and addresses.

"From now on you'll sit at opposite ends of the bus," he ordered.

He placed Devlin at the front because he got off first.

Alexander sat in the back, rubbed his bruised face, and worried what his mom would say. It had been a great day to the start of his new school. He hoped the fight wouldn't affect his reputation.

Worried and tired, Alexander fell asleep. His house

was the last stop on the route, so when they arrived, he was alone. The bus driver woke him up. He rubbed his eyes, stretched and remembered the fight and how he must look. He rubbed his bruised cheek, picked up his backpack and was about to get off the bus, when the bus driver spoke.

"Listen, I heard what that Mr. Ratner said to you, and it was awful, but you got to learn to control your temper, kid, you hear? And get bulked up so the bigger kids won't mess with you. Got it?"

"Yeah, I got it," Alexander replied, still drowsy and only half-interested.

"You got a whole life in front of you, Mr. King. You got an opportunity at this school that's going to put you places you didn't ever think you could go. Understand? Don't throw it away on a stupid kid who doesn't know what he's talking about."

"I know," nodded Alexander.

"Good, now get off and get some sleep. Take a shower and make sure to take care of those cuts. By the way, I'm Robert, Robert Stoneman, but you can call me Bob."

Alexander smiled. "Hi Bob, I'm Alexander... but you can call me Alex."

"Will do, Alexander. Alexander King, huh? That's a great name. Like Alexander the Great."

"Yeah, I wish," said Alexander.

"Don't you worry son, you'll get there. Tell your mother to talk to me if she has any questions about today. I may have to let the school know before they hear about it from someone else, okay."

"Yeah, I understand. Thanks Robert."

"Good. Take care now," he said.

Bob watched Alexander go into the house, waved goodbye and drove off. Alexander went to his room and crashed on his bed.

The Greyhound

The telephone rang and rang... Alexander was fast asleep and thought he might be dreaming it. He opened his eyes but then closed them quickly.

BANG! BANG! BANG! "Wake up!!!" he heard. Was he dreaming again or was it the ghost? God, he hated that ghost. Still drowsy, he decided to get out of bed. He slung his feet over and put his feet into his green, frayed Winnie-the-Pooh slippers. They weren't a good fit anymore but he loved them. Stretching, he walked to the door. His mom was on the phone. He must have slept in. Did his mom even know he was there and just let him sleep?

She hung up the phone, and called out, "Alexander! Alexander, are you awake?"

"Yes mom, yeah, I'm up!" he shouted.

"Can you come down honey? I need to talk to you about something," she said.

Alexander bit his lip. He hoped it wasn't about the fight with Devlin.

"Okay, be down in a sec."

He ran to the bathroom to look at his bruise, hoping there wasn't any. One look in the mirror and yes, there were two big bruises, one on his forehead and one on his left eye. He was sure his mom would ask about them. Slowly he made his way downstairs and saw that his mom had just put the phone down. She winced when she saw his face, then smiled with a touch of sadness. He sat down at the table and faced her.

"Two things," she began. "I talked to Professor Finley and he said you are a very intelligent boy. You answered a very difficult question."

"Oh yeah, the one about gravity," he replied.

"Well you really impressed him, and he told me that he will challenge you more, so you can demonstrate just how smart you are.

"Great," said Alexander sarcastically. How hard would he have to work *now*?

"You'll be fine." She paused. "So, you had a good first day. Right?"

"Yeah."

"Listen, I'm sorry I can't behave like your mom in my class." Alexander looked at her, not knowing what to say.

"If that makes you uncomfortable, perhaps you should switch to another class?"

"NO!" yelled Alexander, near tears. "No! Why? Now I can't even be in your class? I don't know why you made me go to this stupid school. I hate it there."

"Is that why you took it out on *Devlin Ratner* and hit him in the face? I know he hasn't been nice to you, but that's no reason to *hit* him! I heard that he tripped you and you hit him. I just got off the phone with his father and… "

"What? That's not true! It's a lie! He pushed me down the stairs earlier in the day. Rebekah saw it. Then on the bus he held me down on the floor and said that daddy killed himself because of me, or that dad is still alive and has a family somewhere else! I punched him 'cause he deserved it. Robert, the bus driver saw the whole thing. He said you could ask him if you want."

"Okay, Alexander. I'm so sorry he said that, but you'll have to talk to the Headmaster, Dr. Drisdin, about it. He's not very understanding, but I talked to him about the incident and he wants to talk to you both to explain what's expected of you as students at Forrestville Academy. He doesn't want it to happen again. I'll talk to Devlin's father and tell him your side of the story?

"Talk to Bob first," Alexander said.

"Okay, I'll talk to the bus driver first then I'll call Mr. Ratner." She took a breath. "But you have to understand that no matter what anyone says to you, you *can't hit them*. You could get kicked out of school, Alexander. Do you understand? This is a very strict school and will not tolerate fighting."

"I understand! But he pushed me down the stairs!"

"Well I'll talk to the Headmaster." She took a moment and gathered herself. "I want you to know that I'm very proud of you, but I want you to adhere to the rules and no more fighting, okay?"

"Yeah, I got it. I know," he said sharply. "I'm going upstairs. I don't want to switch English class. You made me go to this stupid school. At least you can let me be in your class."

"Okay Alexander." She looked toward him as he

trekked upstairs. "Take care of the bruises. Put on some antiseptic cream. I love you Alexander. Remember that. Remember that what Devlin said is *not true*. Your father loved you very, very much. Still does… He's with us all the time in our hearts."

Alexander turned around but just stared at his mom. He went to his room and buried his face in the covers. He fell asleep and began to dream.

He was Captain Bluewater on a boat in the ocean in some different world and he was looking for enemies. These dreams were very powerful. They gave him courage. He was glad he remembered the details. That was because his father was in his dream, flying a black no-name spy jet above the mountains and castles of Transylvania. The plane dived toward the Black Sea near one of the small Middle Eastern countries always plagued by wars. As the plane flew above him, Alexander gave a thumbs up, but he saw that there were several jets on his dad's tail. His dad made a sharp turn to avoid an attack, then he flew low above the ocean and disappeared. Next, he saw his father ejecting from the plane into the water, and swimming towards a fishing boat to safety. Once he got to the boat, he hung on to the side.

His dad was immortal, so it was easy for Alexander to believe that he was alive and in hiding.

*   *   *

Next morning Alexander woke, showered, dressed,

and went downstairs. While he ate his Honey-Nut
Cheerios, his mom told him that he and Devlin would
meet with the Headmaster during the first period. "Dr.
Drisdin wants to speak to *both* of you and doesn't care
who started it. What matters now is that it won't happen
again." Alexander wanted to tell his side of the story,
and he hoped that Dr. Drisdin was as open to listening as
was Professor Finley.

At school, Alexander and his mom made their way to
the main building. Alexander looked forward to passing
through the lobby so he could see Mr. Harkens' portrait.
At the Main Hall his mom left him but said she'd look
for him during lunch. Alexander entered the large
wooden doors and stepped on cream colored marble.
People were looking at his face. He wondered if they
knew about the fight. He spotted Devlin, sitting on the
black wooden chair right under Mr. Harkens' portrait.

"Poor Mr. Harkens," Alexander thought. When
Devlin noticed him he made a mean smirk. Alexander
sat at the other end of the room and tried not to look at
Devlin but did notice that he too had two large bruises
on his face. Man, he hated Devlin and his stupid smirk.

A woman in her late 40's came out of the
Headmaster's office. "Dr. Drisdin will see you boys in
five minutes." They each said thank you. He felt
awkward.

Alexander glanced around. He noticed the other
portraits hanging in the lobby, but none seemed to be as
interesting as Mr. Harkens. He stared at the portrait. It

was very dynamic.

"Making friends?" said Devlin, pointing at the portrait. His smirk was intolerable. Alexander was feeling annoyed, until he noticed that the Harkens portrait was smirking too, looking the same as Devlin. Alexander chuckled. This was funny.

"What's so funny?" Devlin demanded. He looked up at the painting, but the smirk was gone. Alexander laughed.

"Nothing. Nothing," he glared at Devlin.

"What a weirdo..." said Devlin, rolling his eyes and making a sour face. Mr. Harkens slowly adjusted his face back into its original form. William Harkens looked down at Devlin, then looked over at Alexander who couldn't wait to see what he would do next. Harkens rolled his eyes and puckered his face just like Devlin did. Alexander was about to crack up but Mr. Harkens put his finger to his lips, warning Alexander to shush. Alexander bit his lip. It was hilarious for Alexander to watch this highly respected man mock Devlin. Devlin stared into space, with an occasional glance at Alexander, who was trying hard not to laugh. Devlin crossed his arms and rolled his eyes, which Harkens imitated. Alexander burst out laughing, and that was it... Devlin begun to yell: "What's so funny weirdo? Think it'll be funny when I bash your face in again?" He was yelling as the Headmaster poked his head out and heard him. He shook his head and went back into his office.

Alexander felt relaxed and happy. Harkens continued to mime Devlin's ranting and it was all Alexander could do to not fall off his chair with laughter.

"My dad knows the Headmaster well and I've known him since I was a kid. We often vacation together on Fish Island. I can get you kicked out and your mom fired." But no matter what Devlin said, Alexander continued to laugh. Mr. Harkens was ridiculing Devlin's every gesture and facial expression.

The secretary returned. She had contempt in her eyes when he looked at Devlin, and announced, "Dr. Drisdin will see you now." Harkens looked at the secretary and puffed up his cheeks, imitating the secretary who was fat.

Alexander was having fun but now needed to get serious. He was about to see the Headmaster! He shot Harkens a look. The man's face froze and winked at him just the way he did the first time Alexander saw the portrait. Was he saying, "You're protected?" Alexander knew that everything was going to be okay and he smiled.

The two boys walked into the office, and a tall, lanky Dr. Drisdin greeted them. He was very friendly to Devlin, like they were buddies. He shook hands with the two boys and asked them to sit down.

"Listen," began the Headmaster, "I'm not here to accuse or punish *anyone*. I'm concerned about the incident and spoke to Professor Finley about you. Alexander, Professor Finley was surprised by your intelligence and found you to be a very thoughtful boy. So, we were both surprised that you would start a fight on the bus. When I first heard about the incident, I considered expelling you both. You both have to learn diplomacy and how to stop a fight once it's begun. You need to watch your mouth!"

"But I didn't start it!" exclaimed Alexander. "It doesn't matter, forget I said you started it. It's irrelevant!" said Dr. Drisdin. "I just want to make it crystal clear that it can never happen again. A physical fight is a violation of everything we stand for in this school. He paused, adjusted his glasses, and took a deep breath. "You were brought here to Forrestville to learn civility; to learn ways to defuse conflict and solve problems thoughtfully. There's no strength in violence; in fact it's a weakness. You'll learn skills to deal with conflict. And if you want to stay here, you'll *have* to learn them.

Dr. Drisdin stood up, went to the window and stared for a quiet moment at the campus. Turning back, he said, "Anyway, I'm not going to say anything more, but that if this happens again, you **will** be expelled. Do you understand?"

Alexander and Devlin nodded and whispered, "Yes."

"Good," said the Headmaster.

There was a knock at the door. Surprised, Dr. Drisdin excused himself and opened the door. Two older gentlemen walked in. One was Professor Finley! Alexander didn't recognize the other one. Professor

Finley was about to speak when the Headmaster interrupted him.

"You came at a good time. Our meeting just ended."

"I have something I'd like to say to Mr. King!" erupted Professor Finley.

"No need. I spoke to the boys, and I'm sure this won't happen again," replied Dr. Drisdin.

But Professor Finley wasn't going to take no for an answer. "I want to let him know how terrible it is that someone like…"

"James," Dr. Drisdin cut him off, "I'm taking care of the situation, and I'd be happy if you and Mr. Ratner left the room while we finished up. We can talk later."

Alexander understood that Mr. Ratner was Devlin's dad. He watched him nod to Devlin in support. There really is a conspiracy against me, Alexander thought.

Professor Finley stopped at the door. "Fine," he snapped and glared at Alexander. Alexander stared back, but Professor Finley didn't turn away. Alexander turned his head, but Professor Finley continued to glare before turning to leave along with Mr. Ratner.

"You're dismissed," said Dr. Drisdin. "I don't want to hear about anything like this again. Do you understand?"

The boys nodded and left the room. Alexander determined to get to the bottom of why these two men had come to the Headmaster's office. It was certainly odd that everyone was this angry over a little fight between two new kids. They wanted him expelled!!

Why? Did they know something about him that even he didn't know?

As he was leaving the building, he looked up at Mr. Harkens' portrait, but with so many people around he didn't see any movement. He knew that Mr. Harkens would take care of him. As he moved towards his classroom, he looked back one more time and saw a smile cross the portrait's face, and a nod, as if to say, "Don't worry. I have your back." Alexander smiled. He was satisfied.

*   *   *

Alexander was dreading Professor Finley's class later in the day and worried about it during his other classes and throughout the day. He worried about what he would do. Would he embarrass him in front of his classmates? Would he ask him to stay after class? What would he do? What could he do?

When the time came, Alexander walked into Finley's classroom and a lot of the kids stared at his bruised face. Some pointed and snickered. Kids can be mean. Alexander ignored them and sat down and stared out into the courtyard. When Professor Finley burst into the room he immediately proceeded to teach the class.

This class was on the origin of the planets. Alexander remembered the first lecture and had also read up on the planets and galaxies in his dad's books in the library. When he didn't understand something, he would look it up in Wikipedia. The lecture was starting to bore him and he turned his attention to a large gnarled tree outside the window. He was enjoying watching this tree. He thought about building a tree house and living in it. He would enjoy the birds chirping and would help them build nests.

Perhaps he could be a bird. How much fun would it be to be a bird?! No one would call him short or ugly or stupid, and no one would be say mean and nasty things about his dad... because his dad would be a bird too and they would fly together and be free.

God he's starting to hate being at this school. If he were a bird, he wouldn't have to go to school and deal with Professor Finley, Dr. Drisdin, Mr. Ratner... None of them would matter at all.

"Our sun is only 4.5 billion years old!" his attention was brought back by Professor Finley voice. Alexander really couldn't care less. He'd rather think about life as a bird. He heard the birds calling to him, inviting him to join them in the tree. He stood up and hopped on the windowsill, and then, as if it were perfectly natural, spread his arms and flew out the window. He flew towards the tree where the birds were perched waiting for him. They were happy and he would soon be singing with them.

Alexander saw that his feet were now birds' feet. He landed on a branch and was able to grasp the branch easily. He chirped right along with the other little birds, and they chirped back in a chorus that Alexander thought was the most beautiful music he had ever heard.

He was so happy. He took flight again and flew over the schoolyard, soaring high, then dipping his wings and diving toward the earth. He flew all over the playground and through the jungle gym. He flew high and dived down, and just before he hit the ground he spread his wings, caught the air current, and was lifted back up toward the sky. For the first time Alexander knew how freedom felt. To be free of worries, free of problems of any kind, free of people who were always telling him what to do or where to go, and especially free of kids who called him names and made him wish he'd never been born.

Alexander landed back on the tree branch and resumed singing along with the birds. He was among friends. Friends who would always be there for him to cheer him up when he needed to be cheered up, to help him overcome his fears of failure, and to make him feel good. He continued his chirping.

Suddenly, the birds chirping changed. It got louder and louder, and agitated. It no longer sounded like singing. More like screaming. It sounded like they were trying to warn him of some impending danger. Then, all of a sudden, two birds who had been perched near him began flapping their wings and uttering harsh, very loud "*Kee-ah, kee-kee*" sounds. They seemed to be pointing their wings toward a spot only a few feet behind where Alexander was perched comfortably. He turned his head to look, in time to see two beady eyes gazing directly at him. *A snake!*

While Alexander was lost in his daydream reverie, he failed to notice the snake winding its lithe and lissome body upward toward the branch on which he was happily perched. The other birds seeing the snake flapped their wings wildly and cackled their warning.

Alexander glared at the slimy snake as the creature's forked, black tongue darted in and out of its mouth, and tensed his muscles waiting for the snake to lunge. Then, just in the nick of time and at the speed of light, he spread his wings, pushed himself off the branch like a bullet, and lunged into the air! The snake also lunged forward with such lightning speed and fearsome force that Alexander could feel the ominous rush of air across his face. He could hear the hissing of the snake's gasp as it attempted to bite him; its formidable fangs sparkling with the venom that would have meant a certain death!

Alexander stirred in surprise. He was back in the classroom; his daydream had ended. Professor Finley was hovering over him.

Alexander looked puzzled, until he remembered that just before he jumped off the windowsill in his dream, he had missed the deadly sharpened fingernails on Professor Finley's paralyzed arm. When he quickly and instinctively turned his head, he was saved. Professor Finley was the snake! That whoosh of air Alexander felt was the sound of Professor Finley's limp arm whipping around towards his face! Yes, his dream saved him... Or was it a special force?

Alexander looked at Professor Finley, who was staring at him venomous hatred. It was something Alexander had never experienced or believed to have existed. The kids sat all tensed up, not knowing what to think. They wanted to laugh but didn't dare. Alexander's mother had taught him to meditate, to breathe deeply when he felt angry or agitated. That's what he was doing now, but it only made Finley angrier.

"Where were you, your highness," Professor Finley barked as he towered over Alexander. "Did you hear my lesson, King?" "Yessir," Alexander said, almost in a whisper. "Then please repeat it for me," Professor Finley ordered.

Alexander was nervous, but he was familiar with the material so began, "You told us, sir, that the earth was formed by billions and billions of particles that began to stick together to form the cores of the planets. You explained that the big bang had caused some of the particles to become negatively and some positively charged. A magnetic field was created in the cores of the planets, and as more and more particles stuck to the cores, they continued to grow larger until they became as big as the planets we know today."

The kids were amazed. They didn't particularly like Alexander, but they had to be impressed by what he said. He may be different from them, but he was a very smart kid.

*   *   *

While Alexander was in class, Mary, his mother, was in the library grading homework assignments. While she worked she also worried about how hard things were for her son at his new school. She looked for her wallet in her purse and found the picture of Alexander and his father. She gazed at a younger Alexander standing beside his father after a nice jog behind their house. They had fun running through the farmland and the forest at the foot of the mountains. Alexander was small and wasn't selected for sports teams, but he was in good physical shape. His father had made sure of that.

But Mary worried if Alexander was still taking care of himself. She was worried because his dad wasn't there to protect him. Since his dad disappeared, she had tried to do her best but didn't always have time. Tears came to her eyes and she put the picture away. Wiping the tears from her eyes, she pulled out another picture. In this one, Alexander was standing next to his father, holding a bicycle his father had just bought him. He loved that bike and they often went on bike trips together through the back roads in the forest and into the valley. One day, a year or two after his father disappeared, Alexander went off on that ride by himself. As he passed the trailer park at the foot of the mountains, three young punks hiding in the bushes attacked him.

"Johnson, get him!" a boy yelled as the three teenagers jumped on the small Alexander. They beat him up and stole his bicycle. He lay on the ground for a while, curled up in a tiny ball with his hands covering his face. He wished they would stop. They did finally, taking his bike. Alexander got up; his clothes were ripped and soaked with dust and blood.

He went back home, ashamed and sad, having lost the bike his dad gave him. He couldn't even tell his dad he was sorry. He was so angry he swore to his mom that he would never allow himself to be beaten up. He learned to fight and his mom knew that it was this attitude that got him into the fight with Devlin. He was now fighting back whenever he was picked on.

She remembered the day his bike was stolen. He came home and washed off the blood and dust even before she saw him. He was badly bruised but didn't complain. His dad had taught him to be brave. Though Mary reported the theft to the police, the bike was never found, and it was shortly after that she heard Alexander's father was missing on a mission somewhere in the Middle East. She hadn't thought of getting him another bike as she had gotten so busy trying to sort out her husband's affairs; waiting for his military pension. The military refused. They didn't know if he was dead or alive. She had bills to pay and was trying hard to save.

The picture depressed Mary. She knew how much Alexander loved that bike and remembered how he got it. Alexander had a Golden Retriever once, that he loved. On a beautiful sunny day Alexander was playing outside with the dog when his dog saw a rabbit and chased it up the hill. He never saw the dog again. They assumed he had fallen down one of the many mineshafts left over from the gold-rush mining days. Or perhaps he had fallen prey to one of the mountain lions. They looked for him, but finally gave up. After that, Alexander refused to get another dog. He had loved his Golden Retriever too much.

One day Alexander's father took him to a greyhound race. The local greyhound races were very popular among the military personnel and Alexander's father often joined his friends. But on this day, he decided to take Alexander. "The greyhounds are the fastest dogs, and can run almost as fast as a car," he told young Alexander, who beamed at the idea of watching the fastest dogs in the world. That was the day Alexander fell in love with these dogs. His father even gave him two dollars to bet on a five-dog combination. Alexander picked five dogs and guessed what place they would come in: first through fifth. He ranked them according to whose name he liked the most. He watched with excitement as the five dogs were put into their "traps" right before they were released. He heard the gunshot and the dogs jostled to get ahead. Their long backs slid around the corners as they bounced into each other, their heads bobbing up and down. Alexander was worried that the dog he picked to be last was inching his way to the front of the line. But determined, he leaned over the rail to get a better view of the dogs and put all his energy into a prayer to win. He mentally pushed his dogs to win and they sped ahead. He didn't open his eyes until the dogs passed the finish line!

"Did I get it dad? Who won?" His dad looked shocked. "Yes, you could say so! You won big time!" Alexander looked up at the electronic board showing the placement of the dogs. The greyhounds had reached the gate in the exact order Alexander had bet on! He had won $250.00! So the greyhound became Alexander's favorite dog. That was the day his dad bought him the bike with his own winnings, and he named his bike Greyhound since it was a very fast bike.

But that was then. Now, Alexander didn't have a dog or a bike. Mary knew she had to do something. She went over to one of the computers in the library and started an online search.

The following Sunday Alexander was in bed reading when he heard a knock at the front door. He ran to his window and saw a white truck outside. He went downstairs to investigate, and what he saw stunned him. There were three beautiful, tall, and muscular greyhounds. "All former champions," his mom told him with a big, happy smile.

"mom, this is amazing! How did you… Why did you do this?" he yelled. "Well, I got thinking about when you and your father went to the greyhound race… Remember?"

"Yeah."

"How happy you were and how much you loved it. Then you got your bike and you named it Greyhound. Then your bike was stolen, and your dog was lost.

I went online and learned that until recently, greyhounds that couldn't race were killed. So animal rights organizations arranged to take the ex-racing greyhounds and they were available for adoption. Do you want to adopt one of these dogs?"

"Ummm. YEAH! I would love a dog, mom." Alexander erupted.

Alexander was so happy. He just stared at the three greyhounds, trying to decide which one to pet first. Despite the name, none was grey! One was pure white with a few large grey spots on its back and another spot half-way over its right eye. The other was yellowish with a white face and a white stripe down its back. The last was the color of a marbled dark chocolate brownie. They were all just so unusual and wonderful. Alexander didn't know what to do.

He began to pet the brown one, but then the yellow one came over and pushed the brown one out of the way and licked Alexander's hand. He then jumped on Alexander, knocking him over, and started licking his face. Alexander knew immediately that this was his dog.

"Him, mom. I like him a lot." That was that.

Alexander named the greyhound "Pluto," after one of his favorite planets. Soon Pluto was following Alexander everywhere. Pluto was sad when Alexander went off to school and would wait for him by the door when he came home. He and Alexander would play together in the evening. He was always trying to get Alexander's attention and he refused to sleep anywhere but with Alexander. Alexander was now a happier little boy. He knew that he had another protector. Maybe Pluto could protect him from Professor Finley… and maybe even from the ghost upstairs!

Alexander had a new good friend!

Archons and Nikons

Alexander couldn't catch a break. School was becoming a horror. He was doing as well as could be expected and was a very smart and clever student. But Professor Finley was a different story. He was giving pop quizzes to students at will and the class was subject to these quizzes three times this week alone. They were getting harder and harder and although Alexander prevailed through it all, he wondered why he was being picked on so often. It must be a vendetta. But he looked forward to going home to play with Pluto.

His mom was making friends with his teachers and they talked to her about him. That made him uncomfortable because it was none of their business. One of his teachers, Ms. Simmons, heard about Alexander's fight with Devlin and suggested to Alexander that he should consider "bulking up". She told him about a doctor who helped her nephew who was also small for his age, by putting him on a diet that helped him grow taller and stronger.

His mom said, "Ms. Simmons said that her nephew was even smaller than you. In fact, he was so small, his mother bought his clothes in the children's departments. When they took him to Doctor Schaller his life changed. Doctor Schaller put him on a healthy regimen, and he began to grow."

"I'm fine, mom!" Alexander responded, exasperated. Why couldn't she leave him alone? He knew she wanted the best for him, but she just couldn't understand that whatever she did would only make things worse. The kids would pick on him for not eating the food in the lunchroom, so it didn't matter; they would find something for which they could pick on him and make fun of him. Nothing would change that.

A few days later, despite Alexander's protests, Mary King set up an appointment with Dr. Blair Schaller. Alexander wasn't at all convinced that he could help him grow, but his mother insisted that they should at least hear what he had to say.

Next day, Alexander got dressed, ate breakfast, and ran quickly to the car as it had started to rain. When they got to the office Dr. Schaller greeted them. He was a tall man with dirty-blond curls on his head, much like Alexander's. He also wore thick Buddy Holly-like glasses, which Alexander thought was cool. The doctor reminded Alexander of himself, only bigger and older. He was nice; checked some medical records and examined Alexander. He sat down next to him and said, "You're a fine young man, Alexander." Not hearing nice things said to him, Alexander looked surprised. "You're very strong and healthy. I think you're just a late grower." Dr. Schaller looked over at a big chart. He furrowed his eyebrows and deep in thought, he continued: "Let's see… yes! I think you'll start growing soon if you follow my advice. You'll have a growth spurt a little later than the average boy your age. But don't worry; just continue to stay healthy and positive."

"You think I will?" Alexander whispered… His throat was dry from nervousness. The doctor nodded his head and smiled. "Absolutely. Are you eating lots of vegetables and fruit?"

"No… unfortunately," said Alexander. He didn't much like vegetables.

"It's important that you eat well. But stress and sadness will stunt your growth," he explained, looking him right in the eye. "You know, kids who have higher stress levels and are malnourished grow slower."

"That makes sense," Mary agreed, very interested about everything the doctor was saying. The doctor continued, "You need to eat a balanced diet, Alexander. Drink your milk and eat cheese, so you get the calcium your bones need. Don't eat too much sugar, cake, white bread, muffins rolls, pastries, pasta, white rice, and other bad carbohydrates… your body absorbs them too fast and they give you a sugar-high, so it's not healthy. You must eat what we call *complex* carbohydrates, like fresh fruits, and vegetables, and grains like wheat, oats, and rye. These are good carbohydrates because they break down slowly in your stomach and give you a steady blood sugar level. These are called low glycemic index carbohydrates. They give you a steady energy level. You'll feel great and you'll perform better in school, in sports, in fact in everything you do. Do you understand?" Doctor Schaller looked at him.

"I think so," he said. Alexander was trying to take everything in but was still a bit skeptical about eating things that didn't taste good.

"You should know," said Dr. Schaller, "that fruits and vegetables contain vitamins like vitamin A, B and C; these are the vitamins will make you smarter. You may also need to take some of these vitamins as supplements. The most important vitamin is the so-called "sunshine vitamin" -- Vitamin D. The cells in your body, including your brain, are torn by the environment and all the bad stuff we consume, and they create what we call *free radicals*—cells and other microscopic molecules that destroy your healthy cells and your DNA. We need to get rid of these free radicals by eating healthy. Avoid processed foods like hamburgers or soda because they destroy your DNA. These small, but very important DNA strands, the so-called telomeres, will start to fray like the ends of your shoelaces. But if you eat right and take all the vitamins I'm suggesting, the damaged DNA telomeres will heal and look like new shoelaces. When the DNA is repaired, it will fuel the growth of healthy cells."

"Wow, I didn't know," said Alexander. He didn't know that what he ate mattered much. "If that stuff was so bad to eat, then why do so many people eat it? And why do they sell it?" he asked.

The Doctor smiled, "That's a good question. Because it's cheap, easy to make and they make money. What's most important is that you eat healthy. It will make you smart and strong and your brain won't slow when you get older. I'd like you to eat fruits like blueberries, açai berries..."

"What was that last one?" asked Alexander.

"Açai berries? It's pronounced *ah sigh ee*. They grow in the Amazon jungle! Like blueberries, açai berries are rich in things called *antioxidants* and *anthocyanins*. They, like the vitamins, battle and destroy the free radicals so they can't hurt your good cells. There's even a berry few people have ever heard of, called chokeberry, or 'aronia' berry. It's quite a powerful little fruit. If you see it, definitely try it out. Just about every fruit and vegetable has tons of antioxidants, which can help prevent cancer and all sorts of diseases and will help you stay healthy. Fruits with the darkest colors are usually the fruits that have the most vitamins and antioxidants. They are better for you. Alexander, it's important that you learn more about the food you eat if you want to live a long and healthy life. You do want that, don't you?

"Yes," said Alexander, who was now more interested in what the Doctor told him.

"Well then you have to look on the Internet and do your own research about the foods you eat. Get to know what's good for you and you will find many you'll like. You'll be healthy and happy. Definitely drink lots of milk. It will stimulate your growth. Don't believe everything people tell you. Do your research, okay?"

"Yes, I definitely will," said Alexander enthusiastically. "And sir," he continued, "I did read that drinking lots of milk helps you grow taller. The

Dutch people are the tallest in the world because they drink a lot of milk and eat milk products. Is that true?"

"Yes, that's true. And stay positive and feel good about yourself. I know your classmates aren't always so nice to you, but I promise you that by the time you're my age you won't remember any of it. Just keep telling yourself that it won't last forever.

"Now," the Doctor continued, "are you physically active? Do you exercise?"

"Umm..." Alexander thought and realized that he didn't do as much as he did when he still had his bike. "N-o--- n-o-o-t a-s m-mu-ch as a-r c-a-o-n , I me-e-an sh--hou-ld," he stuttered, his voice going dry.

"Did you say Archon?" replied a surprised Doctor, and looked him deep in his eyes.

"No!" Alexander cleared his voice and sat up straight "What is Archon?" The doctor's look sent a shiver up his spine.

"Very enlightened people. You'll learn about them in school."

Dr. Schaller turned and looked at his mom. "Why don't you get him into a martial arts program? It'll be great for his self-esteem and his overall health."

"That sounds like a great idea, doctor. What do you think, Alexander?" Mary asked her son. "That sounds awesome," Alexander replied, sounding happy and excited. If he started eating well *and* doing karate training, no one would dare mess with him or say nasty things. He was convinced.

"Great," said Dr. Schaller. He grabbed a few bottles of vitamins and handed them to Alexander. "Take these vitamins, eat well, and go exercise. Develop your body and your mind. Be happy, think positively, and you will grow tall."

"Definitely," Alexander responded. For the first time in a long time he felt really excited.

*   *   *

Mary King was so pleased that her 'little king' as she often called him, was getting more interested and excited to learn new things. Alexander did what the doctor told him. He ate well and went on lots of runs with Pluto. Pluto, being a Greyhound, was a lot faster than Alexander, but Alexander did his best to keep up with him and was starting to get faster himself. Pluto often waited for him to catch up. When he did, Pluto started running again.

Mary was pleased that Alexander was feeling better about himself, but she was still concerned that he was always pushed around in school. She heard from other teachers how he was ridiculed for being small and being a nerd, and that he didn't respond because the Headmaster had told him not to.

Mary hoped he wasn't internalizing these insults. Kids could be so cruel and not knowing better, those on the receiving end believed the stupid things their schoolmates said to them or about them. And they wouldn't understand just how wrong they were until many years later. She wanted to get Alexander started in Martial Arts training but didn't know which one. She wanted him to learn to protect himself.

A few days later Mary was the recess monitor in the playground when she saw, in the distance three big boys attack a small boy. She ran over but it was far enough that she worried that the boy might be hurt by the time she got to him. But when she got closer, she saw the smaller boy kick one of the bigger boys and then elbow him across the face. He was then grabbed by the other two boys, he put his hands around the back of one of the boy's head, dragged it sideways and threw him off balance. Then he kneed the other boy in the face and simultaneously elbowed the other boy in the side of the head. Both boys stumbled back and fell to the ground. The first boy got up and picked up a stick and went for the smaller boy. But the little one saw him coming and flipped through the air so that his left foot knocked the stick out of his hand. By the time Mary reached the fight, several students had gathered and were cheering on the smaller boy, chanting, "Ralph, Ralph, Ralph!" The bigger kids were done and managed to round each other up and run off before Mary could identify them. She didn't know if they were students or some local kids who liked to harass Forrestville students. Unfortunately, the students who had watched the fight were not talking. They seemed afraid.

She did talk to the boy and learned that he was Ralph Rivera who was a year ahead of Alexander. She did admonish the cheering crowd by saying that next time they should try to stop a fight rather than cheer it on. They dispersed.

Mary turned to Ralph. "You were amazing. How did you learn to fight like that?" she asked. "Oh, sorry Mrs. King. I didn't want to fight, but they started… and I was just trying…"

"Don't worry about it, Ralph. Are you okay?"

Ralph was relieved. He was really worried that Mrs. King would report him to the Headmaster. He heard about Alexander's fight and the trouble he got into.

"Yeah, I'm totally fine. Just a bit bruised here and there, but I'm okay. Thanks."

"Who were those kids?"

"I'm not really sure," he replied. "I think they were some locals."

She looked at him skeptically.

"Well, let me know if you see them again and we'll file a police report. Now, where did you learn how to fight like that?" Mary asked, "It was really impressive."

"Oh, I've been studying martial arts for a while now at Master Toku's class. Actually, since I was six. He's over in Lake Forest Hills, about twenty minutes away."

"Yes," Mary had heard about him, "I know where that is. Well, what he taught you is very, very impressive!" She smiled. "I'm glad you're okay. Now go wash up before class. I hope I don't see you in any more fights, Ralph. I'd rather you run away and get one of the teachers; all right?"

"Absolutely, Mrs. King. I'm really sorry." Ralph ran off toward the school building and Mary followed. So Master Toku's was the place, she thought. She planned to call as soon as she got home and enroll Alexander in his class.

*   *   *

Alexander didn't see Ralph's fight. As he often did, he was hanging out in the schoolyard near his next class as he wanted to be on time. He liked his teacher of Ancient History, Professor Silversmith. He got to his class and sat in his seat near the window. Before long, he started to watch the birds frolicking in the big tree hugging the window, and soon fell into a daydream. He was a bird again, free from all his schoolmates who were mean to him, free to do what he wanted. He joined the other birds and flew with them far and wide to explore the world. He felt happy.

The class filled up and Professor Silversmith entered quietly but the class jumped to their feet and it was that sound that brought Alexander out of his reverie. He tumbled forward to stand. Professor Silversmith scanned the class like it was a radar screen, moving his head slowly from left to right again and again, as he inspected each student and rested on Alexander. His gaze burrowed into Alexander's eyes, and Alexander felt a "jolt" that coursed through his spine; the same uncomfortable feeling he had experienced when Dr. Schaller looked at him.

"What are they looking for?" he wondered.

Professor Silversmith began, "I have talked to you about the superpowers of the ancient Roman Empire, the Empires of the Celts, the Mongols, the Vikings and the Turks. Those ancient rulers gained power through wars and violence. I described to you some of the great warriors, like Alexander the Great, Genghis Kahn, Julius Caesar, to name a few, who gained power by killing their enemies." Professor Silversmith stopped and looked to see that he had all their attention.

"Today I want to tell you about another empire. An empire that controlled the world more than ten thousand years ago; seven thousand years before we heard about paradise, when Abel killed his brother Cain. This was a world, a great empire, that was led by enlightened people; people who ruled with intelligence, knowledge, wisdom, and compassion. People who were smarter than we are. People who lived in peace and harmony. People of great knowledge. They had advanced knowledge of science that we couldn't match today. They had developed communication systems that provided advanced information about the stars and the sun that we didn't have until just a few decades ago." Professor Silversmith looked up and scanned the room before he continued. "I'm talking about the most enlightened and brilliant people you have ever heard about. They were the **Archons**." He stopped for effect and continued.

"Archons had extraordinary powers over mind and

matter, knowing that these are connected. These powers weren't inherited but were achieved by those who became enlightened after dedicating themselves to the study of philosophy and the nature of the world. Like all the great enlightened beings throughout history, they developed the six universal supernatural powers, which Buddhists later called *Chalabinna,* and worked toward bettering the human race through meditation and the development of advanced technology."

"At first all the Archons were peaceful and used their intelligence and power for the benefit of mankind. As their power increased and as some of the Archons developed magical powers through their study of reality, their power became personal instead of universal. This attachment brought about a separation, like good and evil. Those Archons who were taken over by greed started to use their power for selfish purposes, no longer working for the betterment of mankind. They worked only for themselves. They became power hungry. They separated themselves and called themselves **Nikons**."

The Nikons were now a race with magical powers and they saw the rest of the human race as inferior and non-deserving. Only they themselves deserved freedom from suffering.

The humans and the Archons who did not prostrate themselves before the Nikons deserved to be punished for their lack of celestial vision. The Nikons decided that to teach them they had to conquer them and force them into submission so they built a magical army of

Nikon warriors and waged war on the entire world in 7600 BC." Professor Silversmith paused and took a sip of water. He saw the mesmerized look on the faces of his young audience.

Alexander's mind was spinning.

Why had Dr. Schaller mentioned **Archons**? Was I myself an Archon? Were Dr. Schaller and Professor Silversmith Archons? Were they looking at him to see if he was one of them? Was he an **Archon** or a **Nikon**? Was he good or evil?

Alexander's attention was back on the lecture as Silversmith continued, "The *truly enlightened Archons* at first disagreed and tried to persuade the bad ones, the Nikons, to stop, but as more and more enlightened Archons developed magical powers, the Nikons conquered them with their violent and fearsome warriors, and enslaved them. So the Archons eventually lost their control over the Nikons."

"As the Nikons waged war and destroyed humans who resisted their power, the twelve most powerful remaining Archon leaders knew this could not go on. They knew they would have to combine their powers to stop the slaughter the Nikons were bringing to the world.

They went into their temple and sat there meditating for hours. The earth trembled, the waters rose, and the entire Nikon perverted civilization was destroyed. The few Nikons who survived this natural disaster of earthquakes, volcanoes and floods, scattered throughout the world. They were smart and created many of the ancient evil empires and fathered the evil dictators and empires that exists today."

Professor Silversmith stopped and sighed before continuing. "The last twelve Archon families split up and went into hiding to avoid being targets from evil. They kept their knowledge secret so that it couldn't be used for evil again. Each of the twelve families went to different parts of the world, staying under the radar."

Alexander was starting to really worry, and listened intensely.

"It is believed that where the Archon families lived civilization flourished," Professor Silversmith continued, "They became the brains, the dominant force, behind the earlier Egyptian civilization, provided the wisdom of the Persian, Greek, Asian and Roman Empire's culture and educational supremacy. They are also believed to have been the force behind Atlantis and because of their knowledge were able to escape before Atlantis was destroyed."

And then came the final truth that worried Alexander. "The *Archons are still living among us*; many of them are not aware that they have this power. It is believed there are twelve hidden worlds on or around the earth, all with secret societies whose knowledge, cultures and technologies are far more advanced than ours. They might be in control of many of our powerful good leaders and advanced societies. They are continuously hiding from the evil Nikons, but they know their whereabouts. They are working behind the scenes towards the destruction of the Nikons; to wipe them and their evil away and create the peace and prosperity the world deserves."

Professor Silversmith was making circular motions like a conductor. He definitely had the full attention of the class, most especially Alexander's.

Wow, thought Alexander, was Professor Finley a Nikon out to destroy him? Am I an Archon? Do I know too much? Maybe his dad went into hiding because of the Nikons and one day will come back to destroy Professor Finley. That must be it, he was sure.

"This is how *arête* in Greek came to mean excellence whereas *nikao* means conquest. Prophecy says that one day the Archons will have to come out of hiding, to destroy the forces of evil and find a compassionate and true king to lead them," Professor Silversmith exclaimed.

The students were so spellbound that when the bell rang to mark the end of class, no one got up to leave. When they finally rose to leave, they were very quiet. There wasn't the usual yelling and pushing.

Master Toku

Alexander was very excited about starting his karate training. It was nothing like he had ever done, and he had no idea what was in store for him. When he was alone he fantasized about how powerful he would be with karate training under his belt, so to speak... How he would easily crush Devlin Ratner if he said anything to him or made fun of his missing dad.

It was Tuesday afternoon, the day before his lessons were to begin. When he got home from school, he decided to do some research on the Internet. He watched some martial arts videos on YouTube and got all psyched up. Inspired, he went down to the living room to practice some of what he saw. He moved all the furniture to the side and created a large space in front of the fireplace. Satisfied that this was a good spot, he called to Pluto to come.

The dog raced in from the kitchen and stopping at the door he gave Alexander an endearing look. "Did you try to break into the cupboard for your treats again?" asked Alexander.

The dog lowered his head slightly, which was as good as a verbal admission. Then he looked at the empty space in the room and at Alexander for an explanation.

"We're going to do battle," Alexander said, and using charade-like miming he proceeded to explain what he wanted him to do. He started by wrestling the dog, then told him to sit on the opposite side of the rug.

"Are you ready?" he asked the dog, who sat poised on the rug with the kind of competitive focus that only a greyhound could muster. The white spot above his yellow eye socket moved when he squinted.

"This rug is our ring, red because of the blood spilled over the centuries in Gladiator Tournaments," Alexander announced in a grand voice. Pluto crinkled his brow. He didn't approve of Alexander's melodrama.

"Oh hush," Alexander said dismissively. The dog squinted and arched his back, ready to pounce. Alexander turned sideways, separated his legs, and squatted. He raised his hands, held them out in front of him and curled his fingers over his palms, resembling something between a parrot and a skinny cat. Staring into Pluto's eyes, he shouted, "Begin!" and the two began to clash.

Pluto stood on his hind legs and towered over Alexander. Bewildered, Alexander stared at the giant dog, who jumped and knocked him over. "No! Get off!" pleaded Alexander who was pinned under the large greyhound like a small rabbit. "That wasn't fair!" Adding insult to injury, the eighty-pound dog began to lick Alexander's face. Finally, after about a few minutes of canine slobber, Alexander gathered the strength to push the lovable greyhound off him.

"Way to gloat. I want a rematch tomorrow," he said with a frown. Pluto wagged his tail.

Next day, Alexander was even more excited to start his karate lesson. The school day dragged on. Devlin

Ratner's digs and taunts in Professor Finley's class didn't bother him. Alexander fantasized about what he would soon be able to do to Devlin. Professor Finley, as brusque as always, showed a clip from a documentary on particle physics called, "What the Bleep Do We Know?" The class, including Alexander, loved it. At the end of the clip, Professor Finley asked Alexander some very difficult questions, snorting, "There's a lot to learn, Mr. King, so pay attention."

"Yes Sir," Alexander answered. He was getting better at handling Professor Finley's craziness. Even that didn't bother him now that he had his karate lessons to look forward to.

After school, his mom drove him to the martial arts studio. When Alexander walked in, he saw a modest studio with a boxing ring and a lot of nooks and crannies in which people could train. Alexander saw four older boys fighting with wooden sticks in one corner, and in another he saw two muscular men fighting with knives.

"That's Escrima," a voice called from behind him. Alexander turned and saw a large, muscular Asian man with close-cropped hair in a white outfit with black stripes and a black linen belt tied around his waist. His name in English was inscribed on one end of the belt and his name in Japanese, on the other.

"Are you Master Toku?" asked Mary.

"Yes, I am. And you're... Ms. King?"

"Yes. How are you?"

"I'm good. And you?"

"Can't complain," she said with a slight shrug.

"This must be Alexander?" Master Toku said, a big smile spreading across his face. "Alexander King. Well you've got a lot of work ahead if you want to be a warrior like Alexander the Great, don't you?"

Alexander smiled shyly.

"I saw you noticed the sticks. That's called Escrima or Kali. It's a fighting style from the Philippines. If you train here, we'll teach it to you," said Master Toku.

"Wow," Alexander said, looking at how fast the boys were spinning those sticks at each other. *Rap pap pap. Rap pap pap.* It seemed inconceivable that anyone could move that fast.

"We train in all sorts of styles, from all over the world, including Goju Ryu, which is how I was trained as a boy in Japan, and also Muay Thai and Brazilian Jiu Jitsu. These are our more popular classes. Over to the left you can see the Muay Thai trainers."

Alexander looked and saw a slender Asian man demonstrating to four boys how to make a correct strike across the face with their elbows. Next to him was a rather heavy-set man teaching another group of four students how to kick with their shins.

"I know it seems impossible, Alexander, but that slender guy could knock that big guy out in about ten seconds."

"Really?" Alexander asked. He had trouble believing that. The boy was so skinny!

"Oh yes. No doubt," said Master Toku. He gave

Alexander a warm smile. "Why don't you go into the locker room over there and put on the uniform. I'll talk to your mom for a bit, and when you come out you can say goodbye to her. Sound good?"

"Definitely," said Alexander.

"Okay, off you go then," said Master Toku, as Alexander raced to the locker room. There he found a *gi* lying on a bench. He put it on quickly but wasn't sure how to tie the belt, so he brought it out. He walked over to Master Toku and his mother, who was signing some paper. Master Toku laughed at Alexander's puzzled face and at the belt in his open hands.

"Oh, that's okay, Alexander. Master Gladwell, your master instructor, will teach you how to tie it. I work with the more advanced students. But you'll be working with me soon enough."

"Oh, okay." Alexander looked disappointed.

"Don't worry, you'll love Master Gladwell. He's everyone's favorite instructor." Master Toku looked up at the door, "Speak of the Devil!"

Through the door came a man in his late 20s with short spiked hair, ripped jeans, and headphones in his ears. He slung down his gym bag and removed his headphones. He reached out to shake Alexander's hand.

"Is this Alexander King? The same guy who conquered half the world?" asked Gladwell. Alexander laughed. How did Gladwell know his name already?

"Can't be... you're a bit young, aren't you?" Gladwell joked.

"Nope! Alexander the Great *was* young," Alexander joked. Gladwell and Master Toku shot each other a look and smiled.

"Yes, he was. Young like you, and he trusted his teachers," said Master Toku. "Why don't you go into the locker room with Master Gladwell and he'll show you how to tie your *gi*. Say bye to your mom first."

"Bye mom!" said Alexander as she gave him a big hug and a kiss on the cheek. Everyone could see how much she loved him.

"I'll see you in about an hour," she said.

"Okay," said Alexander, excited to begin his lesson.

"All right, King. You're mine. Let's go do this," said Gladwell.

This time, maybe the first time ever, Alexander thought, he wasn't sad when his mom left him. He knew he was in good hands and was super eager to begin the lesson. After all, he had to beat Pluto in their rematch. Gladwell showed him how to put on the *gi* and shot the breeze a bit as some of the other kids started to arrive.

"So, your father," said Gladwell, "he was quite a man."

Alexander looked stunned. "You knew my dad?" Alexander had never met anyone who had known his dad except his mom.

"I didn't know him personally. I was stationed at his base when I was a Navy Seal. He did some of our training. He was a strong, fearless man. Thinking of following in his footsteps?"

"Oh, I don't know," said Alexander bashfully.

Gladwell smiled. He wasn't going to push Alexander too hard.

"Well you came to the right place to start," Gladwell said. "I think your dad would be happy to know that you were working with Master Toku."

Alexander was mesmerized. How did his dad know Master Toku? He was nervous to ask Master Toku just yet but was comforted to know that his dad would have approved of Master Toku. He was so used to kids making fun of the fact that he didn't have a dad, it was a huge surprise to hear how great his dad was!

More students were coming in and Alexander recognized some of them from school. Some were older and a few were his age, but he didn't see any from his classes. He worried about being ridiculed because it was all new to him. He expected to be weaker than the kids who had been training for a while, and he was smaller than the others his age. Of course, he worried about being beaten up, and these kids were stronger and better fighters than the others in school.

To his surprise it never happened. No one made fun of him. When Gladwell introduced him to the students, they seemed eager to meet him. Later, Alexander learned that this was due to Master Toku's strict policy of punishing students for teasing and rewarding students for helping. Master Toku called this an education in compassion, which was a world apart from the class dynamic at Forrestville. In fact, Alexander had never heard the word used by a teacher there. It was as if the teachers didn't care about the kids or had decided that it was out of their control to do anything about it. Ironic, Alexander thought, how it was in a martial arts class that the teachers taught compassion.

When the students came out of the locker room, they were asked to sit down. One straggler came in late. Master Toku made him do twenty-five pushups before he could take off his backpack and put on his gi. There were about fifteen kids in the class; ten boys and five girls. Master Toku began the lesson.

"Stretch!" he said, as he sat down and began to stretch his hamstrings. Master Toku was incredibly flexible. Much more than Alexander. He would have to work hard to become as good as Master Toku.

"It's good to see you all," said Master Toku. "Amber, Robert, Eric, Daphne, yes even you Jacob," Master Toku said smiling at a brown-haired kid in the front with a disheveled look. Master Toku shook his head. "You too, Andrew. Glad you guys came back. Have you been training over the summer?"

"Yes," they replied in near unison.

"Amber, Robert, have you been practicing together?"

A small girl with blond pigtails looked up as did a boy also with blond curls. He looked about a year older than Alexander. Alexander assumed they were brother and sister.

"Yes, Master Toku," they both answered at the same time.

"Good, good. And you Eric? Have you kept up two hundred pushups a day, as I asked?"

A boy about Alexander's age looked a bit sheepish.

"Ummm… I'm trying. But that's a lot of pushups!"

"No pain, no gain, Eric! You said you wanted to get stronger to move to the advanced class, well, you have to show me that you're serious. Put in the work and you'll get there soon," replied Master Toku. He was truly authoritative.

"Stretch!" Master Toku called. The group stretched one leg.

"Now, I hope you've all met and welcomed the new students. And you, the new students, you can ask the returning students anything and they are required to help you. It's their duty. And I hope all the new students have met Master Gladwell. He's one of the finest warriors and a great guy. He'll be your coach most of the time. As many of you know, we have a very strict no-teasing policy here. If you say anything even remotely nasty or hurtful to another student, it is UN-ACC-EPTABLE. Got it? If you do, you will have to do two hundred pushups every day until you can do it for me with no stopping. That's not negotiable is it Andrew," Master Toku called out a red-haired kid at the back of the group.

"No, it's not!" said Andrew, sounding like he'd been at the receiving end of the punishment.

"But it's not all bad. I also have a strict policy for rewarding good behavior. If you show generosity to another student, help them with a strike or block, or help a student get out of a difficult situation at school, your reward will be extra time with me and the advanced group, so you can learn more advanced techniques and accelerate your rank. Switch legs!"

The class switched to the other leg.

"Learning the art of protecting yourself by training your mind and body for readiness is one of the most important learning in life. Your mind controls your actions, so you are not only training your body to become physically stronger, you are training your brain to become mentally stronger. When you train the motor programs in your brain to become more efficient at making your muscles move, you gain strength in every aspect of your life. Training your brain builds physical muscle. Your reflexes sharpen and you'll act faster. You gain speed. If you're attacked, it's that speed that can make the difference between getting hurt, or even saving your life. So this is serious, and now I'll let you think about that as Master Gladwell takes over."

"Thank you, Master Toku," said Gladwell. "Okay youngins, let's get started."

Gladwell stated with a short talk about Martial Arts, telling them to relax and breathe deeply. They would learn to become fully engaged and alert; always prepared for action. He described the meditation position, which they were required to maintain for fifteen minutes following the stretching exercise. They were instructed to kneel and sit back on their heels, and their hands resting on their thighs palms up. They looked straight ahead, eyes either open or closed, and worked to calm their minds and still their bodies.

"Meditation helps to strengthen the mind," Gladwell continued softly. You need a sharp, focused mind on the battlefield. Meditation can free your emotions, so you don't second guess yourself. You can use meditation to empty your mind of unnecessary thoughts. The Samurai meditated for hours on their duels and battles and prepared themselves for fast action and to fear nothing, even death, when it came."

"Shoju Rojin, was a monk who was taunted by a group of Samurai." He continued." They said that while Shoju had superior concentration, it had no practical use on the battlefield. Shoju invited one of the Samurai to attack him with his sword and he would defend himself with a fan with a metal back. The Samurai accepted and attacked from every angle. Shoju blocked each and every strike with his fan. Finally, the exhausted warrior was forced to admit that the monk's meditation practice did give him an advantage on the battlefield. Today, the military and CIA train their soldiers to use meditation to strengthen their minds. It really helps them focus when attacked." Gladwell suggested that they all read a very important book, "The *Unfettered Mind*," which features the writing of the famous Zen Monk Takuan Shoho. It was translated by William Scott Wilson and was addressed to a master of the sword. Shoho describes "stopping the mind" so that it isn't undermined by judgments, thought of the attack, the intentions of others, or your own defense or fear.

"Don't think about what you should do; don't try to guess your opponent's technique; and don't let fear strangle your reactions or hold you back. Let your consciousness become one with your opponent's so that you become a part of him or her; so much so that you can sense the attack before it comes. Don't focus on the attack. A block avoids or absorbs it, but always look, feel and let your mind sense the next action, technique, or movement."

When his lesson was finished, Master Gladwell asked them to begin with twenty pushups and fifty sit-ups without resting between the two.

Next, he yelled, "Up! Grab a ball and run laps around the mat!"

Alexander looked to the returning students for what to do and saw them pick up five, ten and fifteen-pound medicine balls and start running. Alexander didn't want to look weak, so he picked up a fifteen-pound ball and made it for one lap around the mat before he felt like his arms had given out. "Throw it down King!" said Gladwell. "Grab a five and start slow. You'll get there," he said, shaking his head and smiling.

"Down! Pushups and sit-ups. Then pushups with one hand on the ball and one hand on the floor. Then switch for another ten." Alexander had no idea it was going to be this difficult. He felt like he was going to vomit.

"Down, sit-ups! Hold the ball on your chest for fifty

sit-ups!" Gladwell barked.

Alexander didn't get close to fifty when Gladwell called time. In fact, he lost count of everything and thought he was seeing double. "Okay, pick a partner and grab gloves and pads." After explaining the basic stance, Gladwell taught the kids basic kickboxing strikes and blocks and let them practice for another half hour.

And so it went for two hours every other day after school.

*   *   *

It was exhausting, but his mom assured him that his dad would want Alexander to become strong and discipline his mind and body to be able to defend himself.

No matter how tired he was, he always took Pluto out for a sprint before dinner. They would go to the back of the huge rickety house and race as far as they could up the mountain. Alexander would invariably lose, but it was ok to lose to his friend. As the sun began to slip behind the mountain, he heard his mom call him for dinner. Alexander and Pluto walked back to the house, which looked like a terrifying sight at sunset. An orange glow bathed the front of the house and a strange dark glow on the sides. The back of the house was covered with shadows and it looked like the trees were creeping over the weathered gray wood and forming a dark, gnarled lattice over the shutters… like a prison.

Alexander could have sworn that every night as they walked down the mountain he could see a shadow moving *inside* the attic window. Did ghosts have shadows, he wondered. Perhaps it was just a bird flying over, that he couldn't see in the dark.

After dinner, Alexander would start his homework and work until he finished no matter how long it took him. Pluto, a true friend, would stay up with Alexander, and if his good dog's head drooped over his crossed paws, he would wake himself up, shake his head and continue to watch Alexander doing his homework.

* * *

Some of the kids in Master Toku's classes were too exhausted to concentrate on their schoolwork after karate. Alexander thought it was an excuse; that they were just lazy. On the other hand, Alexander felt himself becoming stronger and more alert every day. He was feeling good about himself now. When the kids brushed by him as they went in and out of Professor Finley's classroom, he no longer let the bigger kids push him around. Evan, a big kid, who occasionally tried to block him with his arms, like he did on the first day of school, did it less and less because Alexander would strike Evan on the wrist hard enough so Evan would let go.

"Who did that?!" Evan yelled. He didn't know who hit him, but no one suspected Alexander… that shy little kid with no friends.

Alexander was more confident, even as some of the older kids still ridiculed and bullied him when they passed him in the hall. His big, round, horn-rimmed glasses sitting a bit crookedly under his wild, curly mop, greased with his mom's hair gel, didn't help. and, his hair was divided down the middle. He'd told his mom often that it was one of the reasons kids made fun of him, but she patted him on the head and said, "They're just jealous of you because you're so smart." Fat chance, thought Alexander. They didn't seem jealous, just mean, because he was different. Their meanness bothered him less and less now that he was studying at Master Toku's. There he was accepted, and he had a group of friends outside school. He started to question some of the things his teachers, especially Professor Finley, taught. So, when Professor Finley was mean to him, he brushed it off. He really thought Master Toku's meditations on anger and suffering helped him appreciate that even people like Professor Finley were suffering. After all, he didn't have the use of one of his arms. Though this was no excuse for Professor Finley's meanness towards his students, at least Alexander could acknowledge that this could be a reason. Alexander had read that Winston Churchill won the World War because he told his soldiers to "never give up". Alexander was also determined to never give up.

It wasn't only Professor Finley's suffering that he began to see. Alexander saw it in all the *students*. Whenever one student would say something cruel to another, the student would be hurt and lash back. Then both would be hurt and angry but pretended they weren't.

It seemed that everyone was afraid most of the time. This was craziness, Alexander thought! It was everywhere. He heard Evan make fun of his best friend Brett. He would say nasty things about Brett's family. Then they would attack each other with words, and gang up on other students, forgetting that they had just hurt one another.

Alexander was reminded of what Gladwell told students to repeat out loud often: "Be aware that there are nasty, unkind people in the world and over time, with the right attitude, you will become kinder towards them and their behavior won't affect you." It was true. Alexander could feel a change in his own mindset. He was becoming kinder and what they said and how they said it no longer affected him. He understood now that the hurt people hurled at you came from their hurt and anger and that, unlike him, they couldn't control their emotions. Not to say that he wasn't hurt by their comments. It was nice to think that he was completely impervious, like a smoothed-over stone that nothing could grab hold of, but it wasn't like that. It still hurt, but he knew that how he reacted to the hurt was his choice.

He still had some difficult moments, but he was happier more often and enjoyed even more watching the birds outside his classroom window. And he was starting to make friends in class. Once in a while he got up the courage to speak to Rebekah and her best friend, Christiana. Sure, he was still awkward when it came to starting conversations with them, which usually occurred just before Professor Finlay arrived. He would say something like, "What did you think of the homework?" or "I hope we don't get a pop quiz today," or "Boy, that question 6 was hard, wasn't it?" - even though he didn't think the quizzes were difficult. Their conversations became more regular, but it was Christiana who seemed arrogant and somewhat jealous of Alexander's intelligence.

Neil Pauley was another bright boy in class who tended to answer questions quickly and easily. But it was mostly Alexander who helped out the other kids by explaining difficult concepts to them, and he didn't appreciate when Neil got involved and competed with him. And while Professor Finley approved of Neil and had it in for Alexander although Neil didn't seem to have any opinions or ideas of his own. He would simply listen to others and repeat what they said. He seemed uncomfortable around Alexander and was constantly vying for Professor Finley's attention... good or bad. Of course, he was speculating. He really didn't know...

Some kids really disliked Alexander and sometimes he thought that things were worsening. Devlin clearly hated him, but he had always hated him, and Alexander was used to it. Devlin wasn't particularly smart, so his behavior didn't affect Alexander much now. But Devlin was starting to build a group of evil kids around himself, including Christian Chung. Devlin was called 'The Snake' but Christian was a real snake. Another was Cain Cavoli, whose face resembled a carved pumpkin on Halloween—or maybe more like a carved Spanish onion since it was more scrunched. He had an enormous nose and was nicknamed 'The Nose'.

More kids were consulting with Alexander about the quizzes and tests, one of whom was Rebekah. She was annoyed that Alexander had the correct answers more often than she did. She wanted to be the best and wasn't hiding it. Christiana, or Christi as she preferred to be called, on the other hand avoided comparing answers with Alexander. She preferred to ask Rebekah or would ask Rebekah to ask Alexander. During these conversations about school, Alexander wondered why Neil Pauley would sit by himself and stay quiet. It was strange, thought Alexander, but then Neil was a strange boy.

Alexander was intrigued by a couple of kids he met. They were cousins; Maxwell Cooper and Gregory Livingston. The Coopers were a famous family in Forrestville. Maxwell's dad owned land, shopping malls and several stores in the area. Their grandfather, Peter Cooper had, at some point, owned nearly every store in Forrestville. Gregory's dad was a marine architect. Their families were nearly as old and prominent as Rebekah's. Gregory and Maxwell were very disruptive. They rarely did their homework and preferred to read and copy from Alexander's notes.

Maxwell and Gregory switched desks with Lim, the small, plump Asian boy Evan loved to pick on, and Jake, a rather nondescript muscular kid at whom Professor Finley enjoyed throwing insults. Alexander didn't know why they switched seats, until he saw Lim's stash of candy; everything from starbursts, gummy bears, sour patch kids, taffy, caramels, and Godiva chocolates. He never saw anyone eat so much candy, as when he watched Lim down a handful of jellybeans and nearly explode. This was too gluttonous!

Maxwell must have bribed him, thought Alexander, since Maxwell and Gregory's grandfather owned the largest candy store in Forrestville. Maxwell must have bribed Lim so that he and Gregory could sit behind and beside Alexander and copy his notes and test answers. He didn't know what they bribed Jake with, but knew it must have been something sports-related since Gregory and Maxwell's grandfather also owned the biggest sporting goods store in Forrestville.

After Gregory and Maxwell sat near Alexander, their grades began to improve substantially. Alexander was actually helping them by allowing them to copy his notes even while covering them up sometimes. Professor Finley began to see that there was some foul play going on, and started to quiz Maxwell and Gregory during class, but with Alexander's help, they did well with the answers.

Maxwell tried to bribe Alexander with candy too, but

Alexander didn't accept this. His mom had warned him not to eat sweets, and she taught him not to take bribes nor snitch on others. Alexander was kind and continued to help Maxwell and Gregory without taking favors from them and their marks improved.

It turned out that Maxwell and Gregory had been taking karate classes for two years at the same dojo but in another studio, and one day, after school, Gregory spotted Alexander.

"Hey Alexander," he yelled and came over to him.

Alexander was happy to see his classmate.

"Maxwell is also here," as Maxwell appeared at the door.

Alexander felt that he was on the inside and had friends both in school and outside school. These two boys really liked him.

*   *   *

A few days later, Alexander sat alone at lunch, reading Sun Tzu's *The Art of War*, which Gladwell had suggested. "Hence to fight," he read out loud, "and conquer in all your battles is not supreme excellence; supreme excellence consists in breaking the enemy's resistance without fighting." Alexander was mulling this as Devlin along with his terrible little duo of Cain Cavoli and Christian Chung came over and pushed Alexander off the lunch bench to make room for themselves. Alexander was humiliated as he sat on the floor with his lunch splattered all around him!

Rebekah was still in line and watched the situation. Spotting Maxwell and Gregory toward the back of the line she brought it to their attention. The two dropped out of line and went to help Alexander. Maxwell turned to Cain.

"Were you looking for a place to sit?" he asked.

"Mind your own business," Cain snapped back and continued eating.

In a split second, Maxwell twisted Cain's arm so that the sandwich he was eating flew out of his hands, then kicked him with such force that he fell off the bench and landed next to Alexander. Christian and Devlin looked around them, got off the bench, and ran. Maxwell saw that Christian's sandwich was still wrapped up, he pulled Alexander back on to the bench and handed him the sandwich saying, "Here, Alexander. I think you dropped this." Gregory sat down next to them and grabbed Devlin's untouched sandwich and water bottle.

The three friends sat together quietly and consumed the evil trio's food.

It happened so fast and so efficiently that the students who watched it were in awe. Surprisingly, it all evaded the supervising teacher's eyes.

Alexander now had good friends he could rely on to support him.

The Class

When Alexander returned to class after lunch, the mood of the students was so tense and edgy, a spark could have set off an explosion.

Some just stared and others looked at Alexander sympathetically. Many were looking at Maxwell with admiration and awe, and some glared with envy and jealousy. The class was clearly divided into three fractions: kids who sided with Maxwell and Gregory's side, kids who sided with Devlin, Cain and Christian Chung - the evil trio - and the kids who didn't take sides.

Alexander could feel the tension and sat at his desk, took his books and notebook from his knapsack and prepared for today's lecture.

Maxwell and Gregory were talking about what happened at lunch and Alexander turned to join in. As the 'heroes' chatted they didn't see Devlin attach a rope to Alexander's chair. Soon Professor Yu Kan rushed into the classroom and stepped to his podium as the kids all rushed back to their seats. He scanned the room with intensity, turned to the board, and began writing.

Most of the kids were bad at math, but some were excellent. Forestville Academy had some exceptional math teachers and a lot of scholars had graduated from its very successful interactive system of learning. Professor Kan demanded a lot and commanded respect both from his colleagues and his students. He expected his students to answer tricky questions at will.

One especially smart kid, Albert Newland, was often the first to raise his hand. Another student, Lim Chang, who always sat in the front row with his candy supplies was also good at math. But it was Rebekah Harkens and her classmate Christiana whose hands were in the air most often. They had the answers and were eager to be heard. They were definitely two of the brightest in math class.

Since Alexander was still shy, he rarely raised his hand. He did so only if he saw that no one had the correct answer. But even then, he would do so reluctantly, and would raise his arm slightly. His teachers, however, were seeing just how bright he was. It was as if Alexander had a third eye and would know the answer before anyone else.

"Mr. King, give me the answer," the teachers would finally say when no one responded, and the answer they got from him was always correct.

Some of the kids who sat at the back of a class were less intelligent and only squeezed through exams because of some connection that helped pull them through. There were three kids in the back of the class who were obnoxious and jealous of the smarter kids, one of whom was Alexander. They picked on him because he was small and nerdy with his wild curly hair and big horn-rimmed glasses!

The evil trio, Devlin Ratner, Cain Cavoli and Christian Chung, were lazy and always scheming. Most of the teachers were annoyed with them, but not

Professor Finley who showed them lots of favor.

Christian's father was a local doctor, who had emigrated from South Korea, practiced in the next town but lived in Forrestville, because his mother wanted Christian to go to the Academy. Christian wasn't close to his dad, but nobody knew why.

Devlin's father was a friend of the Headmaster's, so Devlin was allowed to stay despite his failing grades. He could lie his way out of any situation.

The members of 'The Trio' were often referred to individually as, Devlin, the Evil Rat, Cain, the Smartass, or The Nose, and Chris, the Snake. Today the evil trio was out for revenge. As soon as the class started, they started shooting paperclips at Maxwell's team to agitate them and cause Professor Kan to reprimand them. They made a bow by placing a rubber band between their thumb and index finger, bending the paperclips into small arrows, stretching the rubber band with their other hand and letting go. Agitated, their targets made loud noises and caused a commotion. Professor Kan reacted by making them stand in the corner with their backs to the class. When Maxwell was hit by metal clips in his neck, he jumped up and pointing at the Snake, yelled, "Stop it you pussycat or I will cut your snake face in half!" Professor Kan was angry and ordered Maxwell to the corner. With his back to the class, Professor Kan didn't see who the real culprits were. He assumed it was Maxwell and the others who were causing it. Alexander would have to make him see.

"Stop it!" snapped Alexander at the 'evil trio' after another attack, and turning to the Rat, he accused him out loud as the instigator.

"Mister King" Professor Kan shouted with rage and anger. "Mister King, I do not tolerate disturbance in my classroom. Do you understand?" "Ye-Ye-ah" Alexander stuttered, his face blushing. "Sit down!" Professor Kan commanded.

Alexander slump back into his chair not knowing that the Rat had pulled his chair away with the rope. Alexander landed on the floor with a big bang and a loud scream, which was met with laughter from the class.

Maxwell jumped up to help Alexander. Gregory found the rope tied to the leg of the chair, and lifted it up to show Professor Kan. He untied the rope and held it up.

"Whoever did that will be punished!" bellowed Professor Kan. "I will find the guilty person! I will not tolerate this!"

The evil trio was quiet, but Professor Kan knew that the culprits were at the back of the class. Whenever he posed a question to them, he rarely got the right answer.

"Mr. Cavoli, do you have the answer?" Professor Kan grilled, but Cain would just pull up his shoulder, shrug, but didn't answer. Professor Kan got the same empty stare and silence from Devlin. The atmosphere in the classroom was so tense that it could be cut with the proverbial knife.

Finally, the school bell rang, and the students rushed out with such speed that the building shook.

* * *

Alexander was feeling the benefits of the vitamins Dr. Schaller suggested. He was feeling stronger, and more confident. He was also less shy since starting karate classes.

There was a lot of talk about upcoming tests. Rebekah seemed to be upset with him when he knew the difficult answers before she did. She was always striving to be the best. Alexander was happy when she came by his table during lunch to talk to him. He loved the smell of her hair and when her warm breath stroked his face, he wished he had a sister like her.

A short time later, a couple of boys came to his desk from the back of the room. "Get a life, mister," Chris The Snake, exclaimed, "your dad isn't dead. You don't get any sympathy from us. They often say a soldier is dead when he's alive but missing. He may be a prisoner or a dissident. Your dad is probably one of those. He's alive and we're not going to feel sorry for you," Chris exclaimed with a wicked look on his face.

Alexander was angry and would have started a fight were it not for the Headmaster's warning eating at him. Instead, he turned and walked away.

* * *

In the evening after he had taken Pluto for his walk

and gone to his room, Pluto started to bark and they both heard a car drive up the driveway to his house. He snuck into his mom's bedroom to look out the window. He saw a military Humvee stop and his mom talking to two officers. He could overhear some of the conversation.

"There's still no sign of your husband's whereabouts," one of the officer's said. "He was last seen flying one of our spy jets over some Middle Eastern country. We didn't pick up any signs of him ejecting and we have had no word from local governments about the flight. No one has heard from or seen him. As of now we have him as missing-in-action."

"What can I do?" Alexander's mom shouted, upset. By now Alexander had left the house and was standing at his mom's side. He told the officers what the boys had told him at school.

"That could be," the officer said with compassion.

"But because we don't know, we have to assume the worst, son."

The officers stayed to answer their questions then saluted Alexander's mom and drove away. His mom was crying holding a towel against her face and Alexander hugged her until she stopped; then they went back into the house.

From that day Alexander dreamed often, and with intensity, about his dad. He could remember everything about his dreams as if he were being sent messages. His dad was always flying above him in a black phantom jet. Each time Alexander gave him a thumbs-up and the jet disappeared.

The dream was always the same but there were several versions. One was when the plane flew into the ocean, but his dad ejected then disappeared. Then he dreamed that he saw his dad holding on to a fishing boat as it bobbed up and down until it reached land.

In another version he saw the jet plane turn into a submarine. His dad was the captain and was in control of navigating the seas.

*   *   *

Rebekah was now going over to Alexander several times during classes to talk about science. She was smart and athletic as she'd been taking ballet classes for a long time. Alexander loved her company and sometimes made believe that they were related. Rebekah had two reasons for her visits: she was sharing knowledge with Alexander, and she wanted to talk to the handsome Maxwell who was sitting behind him.

Sometime later Alexander received an invitation to Rebekah's birthday party. She invited Maxwell too, but he couldn't go. Alexander was worried about going alone, since he didn't know if he would be accepted into the Harkens' home. Like Alexander, Rebekah was gifted and had skipped a grade, so they were both younger than their classmates.

Alexander checked the Internet to learn more about the Harkens family. He already knew that Rebekah's great, great, great grandfather had founded Forestville

Academy. She had three brothers of whom Jonathan was the oldest, and her favorite. Her dad William Harkens IV was a real estate developer and oil explorer who discovered a gold mine on their land. This was just before Jonathan was born, so he called him, William Jonathan Gold Harkens V. When the twins were born a few years later, and her father had made more discoveries on the land, he called them Jason Pearl Harkens and Joshua Diamond Harkens. And he also gave his wife a beautiful necklace of pearls and diamonds.

Rebekah was born a few years later; and was a surprise baby. She brought her parents so much joy they called her Rebekah Joy, and she became her dad's pride and joy. Having three brothers Rebekah became a real tomboy, but her brothers protected her... the three J's, as she called them fondly.

*　　*　　*

Alexander was told that he could bring his mom to Rebekah's birthday party. Rebekah liked having his mom as her teacher and wanted her parents to meet her. The one thing that worried Alexander was not knowing if any of the mean kids were invited.

This was his first visit to a friend's home, and he wasn't sure if he would know how to behave. He was sure his mom would make him put on some party clothes that he didn't like, but to his surprise she bought him new pair of jeans, a cool red shirt and a blue blazer.

He thought he looked funny with the jacket and his big ugly glasses.

He was pleasantly surprised when Rebekah told him he looked really neat in his red shirt and new jeans, and her mom added that he looked very handsome. Alexander was pleased to meet Rebekah's brothers who were very friendly and treated him well.

"I hear you're taking Master Toku's classes," Jonathan said.

"Yeah," Alexander replied and then realized that he had seen the twins, Jason and Joshua in the sports complex. "I've seen you guys down there," he said.

"Yeah, you probably have," Jason said, "we assist the masters in some of the classes." "And now we have met, we'll look out for you," Joshua smiled, "and we'll help you if we can." Alexander smiled. He felt as if he was gaining a family; a sister and three brothers.

When they went home that evening and he walked into his house, he realized he was enjoying his house and felt safe with Pluto there to protect him. He wasn't even afraid of the ghost.

He would hear the ghost yelling in the middle of the night, "Let me out!" and he would knock on the ceiling in the annex. The yelling got worse when there was a full moon and Pluto would bark at the ghost, which made the ghost angrier and louder. Alexander no longer cared; he was protected by his big Greyhound and he felt closer to Pluto each day. He could hardly wait to get home after school to play with him. They had fun together.

Alexander would go to his sanctuary to do his homework and study, and sometimes during his studies he would take a break and take Pluto outside for a run. He would climb out of his window and climb down on the big tree that reached his room. Pluto would run down the stairs and meet him outside.

Often Alexander and Pluto would explore the neighborhood. Once they faced a snake that was about to attack, but to his surprise Pluto barked at it and the snake slithered away. When he got home, he immediately went on the Internet to learn about snakes. He wanted to know which ones were poisonous and dangerous and which ones weren't. Other kids could ask their father, but Alexander couldn't.

Alexander's home was now his golden mansion... his palace. It was old with so many rooms and nooks and crannies that he was always finding something new. There were cupboards, closets, storage rooms, and even boxes filled with ancient treasures. He believed they were left by the McCoy family.

During one search he discovered his father's gymnasium, a private workout room in the basement behind a secret door. He didn't tell his mom about it and explored it with Pluto. Using a flashlight, he found that his dad had installed lights, and when he changed the bulbs and attached the wires, he saw a fully equipped gym.

The school bus let him off a couple of hours before

his mom got home. Bob, the bus driver, was very protective of him. Alexander would play with Pluto and have a snack, then he would climb down through a secret floor-door in the kitchen and head down the stairs to the food storage room, where another secret door led to his dad's gym. He enjoyed working out. There was a rowing machine, a stationary bike, a treadmill, weights, and ropes. Alexander cleaned up all the machines, since they hadn't been used for a while, and soon they looked like new. He thought his mom wouldn't want him to use his father's equipment as she wanted everything to be ready for him as it was, when he came home. So he kept the window facing the driveway open and Pluto kept watch, and when his mom's car drove up, he barked, and they quickly ran up to his room. His dad had posted some good charts on the wall that helped Alexander create a personal program that helped him strengthen specific parts of his body. He could see his muscles getting bigger and he seemed to be putting on weight. His legs were developing muscles from bicycling and jogging with Pluto, and together with his Martial Arts training he was making great strides.

* * *

He was doing homework after dinner one day, when his computer screen suddenly turned blue. He thought the computer had malfunctioned until he heard a voice coming from it and saw a blurred figure on the screen. "Hi Alexander, how are you," a voice said. "Don't be afraid. We're looking after you." The figure got brighter and began to look like the man in the moon. He wasn't scared at all. With Pluto beside him and his mom downstairs he felt safe. The voice and the picture were comforting.

"We are protecting you and will be in touch when we think you need us," the voice continued, "We want you to watch a training video. You'll learn a new jujitsu defense technique that you should demonstrate in Master Toku's studio tomorrow! You'll win matches even against your teacher, who has several levels of black belt." The voice and the man's silhouette were gone, and the jujitsu video started. Alexander watched the video several times. It was amazing; simple yet extremely effective.

He wondered how they knew about Master Toku, He was comforted by the advice and that he was being protected and helped. He continued his training and exercises, both at home and at Master Toku's dojo. He watched the video until he was exhausted and fell asleep. He was anxious for his next Martial Arts class. But he would keep these videos and his visitor a secret.

The next day, after school, he arrived at the dojo. Master Gladwell took the class through some hard exercises and showed some new defense techniques. He invited one of the students up "Let me demonstrate this one for you," he said. No one was eager to go up to be ridiculed. Then Alexander stood up and stepped forward.

"I'm ready Sir," he announced.

Master Gladwell asked Alexander to stand in front of him and attack so he could demonstrate a new contra-attack. Alexander bent his knees, moved toward Master Gladwell and confused him by bending down and kicking his left leg. He then twisted around in the air and hit him hard on his right shoulder. His actions landed Master Gladwell on the floor.

The class was amazed at his moves and clapped in excitement. Alexander turned and went back to his place on the floor as Master Gladwell slowly got back on his feet.

"How did you learn to do that?" Master Gladwell asked surprised.

"Just made it up Sir," Alexander responded.

*　　*　　*

Alexander, Maxwell Cooper and Gregory Livingston became good friends. He enjoyed helping them with their homework and gave them his notes before he handed them in to the teacher. They were both doing well and appreciated Alexander's help. They saw each other frequently at Master Toku's studio and took some lessons together. He had other friends too in the studio, including Rebekah's brothers Jason and Joshua. The two brothers would go into his classes to help coach the students.

Maxwell and his cousin Gregory were very popular with the girls. They were great athletes, excellent soccer and basketball players but they seemed to excel at every sport in which they participated.

Rebekah and her friend Christi enjoyed hanging out at their table and would pretend that they needed Alexander's help with some problem. But they just wanted to be around the cousins. As the cousins started to do well in school, their professors became suspicious. Such jocks were important to the school and they needed to do well academically too, but it was Professor Finley who suspected treachery. He often asked them some difficult questions in class to trap them.

"How many planets are circulating around the sun, Mr. Cooper?" Professor Finley would call on Maxwell. Maxwell would be flustered at first, but Alexander had learned some ventriloquist's tricks and would throw his voice in a whisper to Maxwell... "Nine".

Maxwell hesitated, as if in thought, and answered "Nine." Professor Finley tried but always failed to catch the boys out. It made him furious.

"Give me the names of the outer planets, Mister Cooper," Professor Finley would yell. Alexander would throw his voice to Maxwell, one at a time, and Maxwell repeated, "Jupiter, Saturn, Uranus, Neptune and Pluto," pretending to be counting them out on his fingers.

So, it went, day after day, both Gregory and Maxwell triumphing with Alexander's unique skills. Professor Finley finally stopped.

*   *   *

One afternoon Rebekah was sitting with Alexander when she overheard Maxwell and Gregory discussing their exercise routine. "We need to join a gym," Gregory said. "Yeah, we need to do that to stay in good shape. I've made a list of some places we should look at," replied Maxwell.

"Are you guys looking for gym?" Rebekah broke in.

"Yes," they said in unison.

"My dad has a nice gym. I can ask him if you can use it."

"It will probably be too much, and your brothers might not like it," Gregory suggested. Rebekah said she didn't think so, when Alexander chimed up, "I have a gym in my house. My dad built it. Do you want to come and see it?" he whispered, keeping his voice low.

"Do you use it?" Maxwell asked.

"Yes, every day, but my mom doesn't know I go there. I'm sure she wouldn't mind but she wants it kept in good condition for my dad when he comes back," Alexander explained.

"Alexander works out with his ghost," Rebekah joked.

"Do you have ghost in your house?" Gregory asked in disbelief.

"Yes, he has," Rebekah replied and laughed. "He thinks it's an old gold miner who lived there once and hasn't left."

Alexander looked at Rebekah. She could be so annoying and couldn't keep anything to herself. "What are you talking about?" he snapped.

"Hey, Alexander," Rebekah said, "it's not a secret. It's a fact that many of the gold miners' houses are haunted. My dad knows the man who lived in your house before your family moved in. He told my father that he heard the ghost screaming all night, and his wife made him sell the house or she'd have a nervous breakdown. They had to sell the house fast, so your dad got it for a good price."

"Yes, the ghost is still there and as loud as ever. My mom has the TV on all the time to kill the sound," Alexander said.

"What?" shouted Rebekah, "The TV must be annoying you!"

"That whole area on the hills is so interesting, with some of the best architecture around here. The old miners had money and were creative," Maxwell broke in and changed the subject.

"Thank you," replied Alexander.

"I heard that these mansions were connected with tunnels and caves," Gregory revealed.

"The gold diggers would dig tunnels from their houses to the neighbor's and dig for gold. They were very smart and ingenious. They built underground bunkers and caves where they could live for weeks," Maxwell added.

"Yeah." Gregory continued, "my dad often pointed to the small hills throughout the area and said that they were created from the dirt that was removed from the tunnels."

"Much of the land above your house once belonged to the military and I think they still use the tunnels and caves for training," Gregory continued. "But there are also snakes, rats, and other creepies, maybe even werewolves, in there."

"Gosh, you guys know a lot, I can't wait to show you my house," Alexander said quite excitedly.

"Yeah, we'll come up to see it and your gym soon," Maxwell replied.

"It would definitely be cool," Gregory agreed.

The boys looked at Christiana and Rebekah and they looked at each other.

"We don't care for ghosts, so we'll pass," Christiana grinned.

The Secret Chamber

It was an unusually peaceful morning at the old McCoy's place nestled in the neck of the mountain. The creaky old house swayed in the wind; the sun popped its yellow face behind the Forrestville Mountains sending weirdly shaped shadows through the tall trees and onto the 'Golden Mansion' facade. Alexander and his mom were sitting at the round dining room table that had belonged to the McCoy family, having a quiet breakfast.

His mom loved the table and still kept a setting for his dad. She still expected him to walk through the front door, or perhaps come down the stairs having had a good night's rest. If it helped her make it through each day, so let it be, Alexander thought.

"Your dad loved this table," his mom said, interrupting his thoughts and breaking the silence.

"I know," Alexander nodded. "You told me hundreds of times that dad loved round tables. He would say that at a round table everyone was equal. It was more democratic than a square table, where one person sat at the head." Alexander replied, somewhat irritated, because she had disturbed his thoughts. His mom smiled sadly; she missed her husband so much. She always served dinner in the dining room and they often had breakfast there as well. It was their family time together.

Alexander was feeling good today and said, "Mom, can I bring Maxwell and Gregory home one day?"

"Of course!" her face lit up. She was glad he had

found friends at the school.

* * *

A few days later he told his mom that Maxwell and Gregory were coming over and asked if they could stay for dinner.

"Yes, of course," his mom said.

The school bus dropped the three off at Alexander's house after school. Maxwell was excited when he saw the McCoy house from a distance.

"What a great house," he said as they got closer to the big haunted structure.

When Alexander opened the door, Pluto was there to welcome them, barking, running circles around them and trying to jump up to lick their faces. His way of saying: "Welcome, I approve of you both." Alexander walked them through some of the rooms but there were way too many for his two friends to see them all. And so many were still hidden. He was so pleased to have them there and could see that they really liked the house. He took them up to his room, where they were fascinated with his computer and all the amazing stuff his dad had brought back from his missions.

He didn't seem like a nerd to them now. They loved Pluto and were amazed by his German computerized globe. But they kept looking around thinking that McCoy was there somewhere… Though they couldn't see him, perhaps they'd hear him momentarily.

"Is he really up there?" Gregory whispered.

"Yeah," replied Alexander, "but he sleeps during the day and comes out at night."

"That's so weird," as he stared at the ceiling, worried.

"The story is," Alexander explained, "two gold mining brothers, William and Winston McCoy, made a lot of money on their gold mine. They met a girl at the local saloon who was sick, and they nursed her back to health. She stayed with them and they both fell in love with her. The two brothers fought over her, and William fell, hit his head and eventually went crazy. Winston built a room in the annex and locked him up until he died. So his ghost is still here, haunting the house."

Gregory shook his head, "All this for a girl? How stupid!" he mumbled.

"Not that stupid," interrupted Maxwell, "they made a lot of money here and became wealthy, but there was only one girl for about a hundred men."

"Still," Gregory continued, "all this fighting just for a girl."

"Yeah…" Maxwell was lost in thought as they were looking out the window, then erupted excited, "Look out there Gregory!" pointing at a herd of horses and cows at the far end of the King property. There was a lavish mass of trees, and acres of green that ended with a mountain rising majestically on the horizon.

"It's an awesome view!" he exclaimed.

Alexander showed them how he climbed out the window down the tall old tree to the yard. Maxwell and

Gregory chose the stairs and they all went down to the gym. Alexander guided them through the secret kitchen door and climbed to the storage area where he opened a door that led into the gym. They were fascinated by the gym. It was complete with a treadmill, Stair Master, rowing machine, spinning bike, ropes, gym balls, cowbells, benches with dumb bells and old-fashioned iron weight bars.

"Your dad was a serious bodybuilder. He must have been pumping iron and building abs and leg power. Everything is here," noted Maxwell.

"Look at all the gym equipment on the walls," exclaimed Gregory, "your dad knew his stuff!"

Alexander was proud to point to all exercise diagrams on the walls. The kids found gloves that were too big, but good enough, and weight-lifting belts that had to be wrapped around their waist twice to fit. They really felt ready for a good workout.

They worked out for a while, and between each set they explored the room. Gregory found the music system that sounded great, but Alexander turned it off because they wouldn't be able to hear his mom coming into the house. They would need to rush upstairs when she arrived.

When Gregory finished using his iron weight bar, he stood it against the side wall, but it slipped and fell sideways against the back wall that made a hollow sound.

"Hey, did you hear that?" Maxwell asked.

"What?" said Alexander.

"The echo from the wall."

"No," answered Gregory, "but let me do it again."

Gregory picked up the iron bar and knocked it against the wall.

"Yes," they all agreed. There was definitely an echo.

"This must be a separation wall," said Maxwell, "there's something behind this wall," he kept knocking with his knuckles. Then he grabbed the weight bar to tap more of the wall.

"It must be a big empty space... maybe a secret chamber or something," Maxwell guessed. They searched the wall hoping to find a secret door, but they couldn't find one.

"Maybe it's an old closed off gold mine cave," Gregory suggested. Alexander was amazed with the new discovery, but he didn't say anything. They heard Pluto bark, signaling to Alexander that his mom was home. The boys quickly left the gym and rushed upstairs to the living room where they greeted Mrs. King with charming smiles.

"Remember," Alexander had reminded them before the front door opened, "not a word about the gym. We were studying and playing. My mom is a Tiger Mom."

They went up to Alexander's sanctuary to study and prepare their homework for the next day while Mary King prepared dinner. They had a good time and a nice family dinner. Mrs. King had prepared arugula salad with tomatoes and avocado, as well as Chicken a la King with pasta. Gregory and Maxwell hadn't had a meal like this before, and when Mrs. King told them the name of the dish, they laughed and told her they really liked it. Alexander was very happy to have his buddies over. They had dinner at the round table in the dining room and noticed the extra setting for Alexander's dad.

*   *   *

After dinner Alexander's mom drove them to the Martial Arts studio. Maxwell and Gregory had signed up and were taking the same classes, so they were a team! And so it went -- once or twice a week they came to Alexander's house to use the gym, and some days they met at the dojo. When they came to the King house after school they worked out in the gym, searched for tunnels and chambers looking for more secret rooms, then did their schoolwork with Alexander.

"Many old mining houses, especially the bigger ones like this, had caves and tunnels under the entire house leading to the mines," said Maxwell one day. "My father's great grandfather did business with the old gold miners, and my dad was fascinated by gold miners and learned their stories from my great grand-dad. As a young man he had wanted to re-explore the gold mines and find some gold," he smiled, "but my great grandfather talked him out of it saying the only thing he would find was 'faux' gold. It looks like gold but it's junk and has no value."

Gregory and Alexander looked on in amazement as

Maxwell continued to tell them everything he heard from his dad. "The gold miners with the biggest mines had the biggest houses, and many looked like this house, with four rooms on each floor and a large kitchen.

Each miner would have a group of men working for him and they would stay in the house and go down to the secret passages and tunnels every day to continue digging. They would bring the excess gravel and sand out through the house and pile it up outside, these formed the hills that you have near your house, Alexander. Even your driveway is made from tunnel shaft dirt," he explained.

"Gold mining was done in secrecy. If you made a discovery, the other miners would get jealous, so no one knew how much gold the kingpins had assembled," Maxwell continued. "My father thinks that there may be several mine shafts and tunnels leading into your basement, but they are dangerous. They're old and could collapse. And they may be filled with snakes, rats, beavers and all kinds of animals. So we should be very careful when we poke around here," Maxwell cautioned. All this made the young explorers even more eager to look and find!

*   *   *

The next day at school was strange. Professor Finley let the 'evil trio,' the Snake, the Rat and the Nose, hand in a blank test paper. The students had completed their multiple-choice tests at their desks and walked them to

Finlay's desk. Devlin Ratner, the Rat, picked up the trio's tests and went to put them on Professor Finley's desk, but on the way, Albert Newland pulled them out of his hand and saw that they were all blank.

"Hey man, keep your nose out of my stuff; give them to me!" The Rat screamed, but Albert threw the papers to Christi, who handed them to Rebekah, who quickly snapped pictures of the three blank pages. "Give them to me!" the Rat yelled, grabbing Rebekah's arm.

"Get your dirty hands off me!" Rebekah screamed so loud that Maxwell and Gregory jumped up, grabbed the Rat so hard that he fell down and crawled back to his seat like a rat...

Christiana took the blank papers to Professor Finley's desk and placed them on top of the others. They watched as Professor Finley placed them under the pile. He picked up the ones at the top and started to go over the questions, calling out the students' names.

"What keeps the planets in their orbit is gravity. Good." Professor Finley looked at the tests in his hand: "Lim Chang: passed; Mr. Livingston: passed; Mr. Cavoli: passed; Ms. Harkens: great; Mr. Ratner: fine job; Mr. Chung: passed; Mr. Cooper: Ok." Professor Finley continued and finished them all, including the 'trio' – they all passed.

Rebekah's hand flew up, "I'd like to say something Professor!" Professor Finley rebuked her, "Please don't interrupt me." The students who had seen the blank pages shook their heads in disbelief. They knew they had 'DNA proof' of Finley allowing the evil trio to cheat their way through school.

The three friends were in good spirits after school, joking and having fun on the school bus on their way to Alexander's house. Bob, the bus driver, was happy to see how well Alexander was doing. He had his friends whom he treated like royalty. The boys were still jovial when they got to the 'Golden Mansion' and continued fooling around as they made their way down to the gym. The route was complicated. They had to open the secret access door on the floor that led into the storage cellar. The wooden lid was in the cupboard at the corner of the kitchen. Then they had to climb down a steep staircase leading to the cellar filled with refrigerators, freezers and food supply cabinets. They were still laughing and joking when they opened the door to the cellar and ran down the steep stairs. Gregory slipped and swore. Maxwell laughed and called out, "You are so clumsy, you stupid city boy!"

Gregory fell with a bang, and Maxwell following him had to jump sideways so he wouldn't land on him. "You're the stupid one," sneered Gregory. Lying on his back, he kicked Maxwell with such a force he almost flew into the big freezer; the freezer, which was on wheels, smacked into the wall with a loud, explosive bang. "Bing! Bang! Boom!" the sound echoed through the room and opened a secret door. The boys froze in fear and stared toward the black hole from where the sound had come. They were expecting a monster to come out of it.

The freezer had activated a secret button that opened the door to a big, black hole.

When the door opened, the boys jumped back toward the stairs and after they recovered their courage they tiptoed slowly toward the black chamber. Remembering what Maxwell's dad had said about the tunnels and caves being home to dangerous animals - snakes, cougars, bears, raccoons, rats - they were too scared to go further. They ran upstairs to the kitchen and found three powerful flashlights. Each armed with a flashlight, they picked up an iron bar and the three explorers went back down to the cellar and made their way into the secret chamber. It was a large room with cement reinforced walls and columns to support the house. It was furnished with a bed, a table and chairs.

"It looks like a bomb shelter I saw on TV," whispered Alexander, "the type of bunkers used in case of a nuclear attack, hurricane or earthquake. This was probably part of the underground railroad." "Yes, you are right," called Maxwell, as he opened a door to a small toilet with running water.

"Ouch, the water is bloody or rusty," he said as he opened the faucet.

"There's another staircase," Alexander yelled excitedly and saw another door. He climbed up with the aid of his flashlight and found the door locked. "It figures," he said, "who wants some criminal climbing into the house through these tunnels?"

"I wonder if the stairs lead to some place outside the house," Gregory asked curiously.

"I'll go up the stairs and knock on the door, and you Alexander run outside and see if you can find the exit," Gregory yelled, as Alexander climbed back to the kitchen stairs.

"Knock!" he screamed when he got upstairs, but in spite of the knocking it took time finding the exit. Alexander opened a door from the dining room into a coat closet and, hidden behind the clothes, he found the door leading to the basement. It was safely secured with three bolt locks. He opened the basement door and saw Gregory.

"Welcome to my home," Alexander laughed, "Mr. Livingston I presume," he announced as he helped Gregory up. They agreed that this entrance made sense. It was a much easier entrance to the basement than the one through the kitchen. Then they found a door leading into another triangular room. This was the room behind the gym where they had heard the hollow echo.

This room was Alexander's dad's repair and hobby shop. This is where Grigory King had built much of the furniture.

"Your dad has great tools," said Maxwell, holding a set of drills. There were chainsaws, hammers, drills, screwdrivers; every tool a man could want.

Alexander looked through the lockers and boxes stacked up in the corner covered in plastic. There was no direct entrance into this room from the gym. Just as

Alexander was about to look through the boxes, Pluto barked, signaling that Alexander's mom was coming. The boys quickly closed all the doors and rushed upstairs through the kitchen staircase into Alexander's room. They sat down looking like they were deep in their homework and they had begun studying and preparing to do their homework when they heard angry screams from his mother in the kitchen.

"Alexander, come down here! Alexander, come down here right now!" his Mother yelled. They rushed down the stairs to the kitchen.

"Why were you in the cellar?" his Mother asked, still angry. "And why did you move the freezer?"

"Well," Alexander stuttered, trying to find an excuse, "we were looking for a coke and we went downstairs to check if you had any stored away," Alexander continued, more and more anxious as he talked.

"When we climbed down, Maxwell slipped on the steps and fell into the freezer. It moved but we didn't move it back. We didn't want to damage anything," Alexander finished. He knew that his mom was looking for signs that his dad had secretly come back.

His mom smiled, relieved.

The rest of the evening was unusual. There was little talk during dinner. They were all thinking about the day's discoveries.

*   *   *

The next day was another tense one at school, and the

boys couldn't wait for it to end. When the school bell finally penetrated through the air, sending echoes through the halls of Forrestville Academy, the boys rushed out.

Maxwell had gotten permission to sleep over at Alexander's, and the two friends rushed to the school bus.

The yellow bus sent up a dust cloud as it moved along the twisted road. It rattled and choked as if it were a worn-out tractor, and the noise was so loud the boys couldn't hear each other. When they finally reached the house, they ran up the driveway. Pluto barked and jumped happily as they played with him in the garden on the side of the house next to the big tree that reached up to Alexander's room. Maxwell often looked up toward the annex window, wondering if William McCoy's ghost was watching them. He wasn't staying over just because he liked Alexander; he wanted to find out if the house was really haunted.

They went to the kitchen and grabbed a few open sandwiches Mary King had left for them. Then they got dressed in their explorer clothes - blue jeans, sneakers and over-sized T-shirts - and entered the bunker through the closet in the dining room. Maxwell found the light switch, but the bulbs were burned out. Alexander found new ones, replaced them and the place lit up. Now they were ready to explore. They started with the boxes in the corner of the secret chamber, removed the plastic covers and, with some difficulty, opened the first box. All were surprised when they found it filled with military gear. They found special military boots, the type that reached up under the knees and had thick soles for good traction on wet land. Another box had uniforms, gas masks, powerful flashlights with, they believed, self-charging batteries, as their light was still strong.

In other boxes they found ammunition and night goggles, walkie-talkies, telephone radios, and maps. The boys were excited; the radio and the walkie-talkies worked! It was all too cool for the young explorers. They tried on the uniforms, the gas masks, and the night goggles. Turning out the lights they played hide and seek in the dark... the night vision goggles were incredible! They couldn't hide from each other! Then they played with the walkie-talkies.

Maxwell stayed in the basement and Alexander went outside. Outside, Alexander was surprised to see his mom's car pulling up in the driveway. He called Maxwell on the walkie-talkie to turn off the lights and come out. Pluto hadn't warned them.

Maxwell quickly emerged from the closet leaving all the military gear on the floor, closed all the doors and quickly ran up the stairs into the dining room closing the double doors behind him.

Both boys ran to help Mary King out of her car, asking her if there's anything they could bring into the house.

"What are you guys up to?" his mom asked, seeing that they were just too happy.

"We were playing with Pluto," Alexander replied, which was partially true.

The boys didn't have Martial Arts class that evening, so they weren't in a hurry to go in. They took Pluto on a long walk while Mary King prepared dinner. They even had time to go over to the neighbor's and see the horses. Pluto followed along, very pleased with all the attention.

*   *   *

Alexander was happy little boy… He was 11 years old and for the first time he had a real friend and no longer felt that he was alone against the world. Maxwell was different. He was a year older, taller, handsome, outgoing, sporty… and he had a father. Despite these differences Maxwell was a good friend to him, and Alexander really liked Maxwell. Maxwell liked Alexander because he was smart, a good student, and helped him get better grades. And now he was having so much fun at his house, which not only was interesting, but had a great gym.

After a good dinner the boys went upstairs to study and play. Alexander worked on his computer, but Maxwell was preoccupied with the ghost and wanted to know if the spirit of old William McCoy came out every night.

"Have you ever seen him?" he asked.

"I think so. I've seen shadows and I'm sure I saw his eyes shining in the dark," said Alexander.

"Gosh, were you scared?" said Maxwell, clearly nervous.

"Nah, not really," Alexander replied, trying to sound cool. He didn't talk about all the times he had slept under his bed out of fear, or the times he had run downstairs and slept in his mom's room.

It was getting dark and the wind was picking up; the trees and bushes swayed in unison, including the tall tree next to Alexander's window, all sounding like they were talking to each other. The big tree by the window was banging the window and creating a scary sound. Sometimes the knocking got so loud that Maxwell looked seriously scared. Once he actually let out a low scream, "uh ooh!". At about 10 o'clock Maxwell was really getting nervous and started to pace back and forth. The knocking got louder. The branches were attacking the house and the leaves were making trilling sounds like what you heard in scary movies.

*　　*　　*

Maxwell was using his flashlight to look outside the window to make sure that there weren't any creatures outside. He kept stealing looks at the small window of the annex that was the haunted room.

"Can we get up there?" he mumbled.

"Huh?" responded Alexander, who was engrossed in his homework and wasn't aware of Maxwell's concerns.

"I asked if we can get upstairs to look into the window of the annex, the ghost's room," Maxwell repeated.

Alexander came over to the window... The branches

of the giant tree outside were heaving and sounded like they were saying "Hello" to him.

They both pointed their flashlights up toward the annex window.

"I've never been up there," said Alexander.

"We don't have a ladder big enough to reach three stories, and the attic access door in the hallway is locked."

Then they noticed that one of the big tree's branches reached right under the window and formed a natural ladder. Alexander could easily climb out his window by grabbing some of the higher branches then stepping right onto this tree ladder. He could then climb to the center of the tree and down to the ground. He had had the foresight to nail some wooden steps to the lower trunk of the tree to make it easy for him to climb up to his room and vice versa.

*   *   *

The wind was stronger now and the sounds were very harsh and scary. In spite of this, Alexander swung open the window, climbed out on to the windowsill, grabbed the upper tree branches with his left hand and crawled on to the tree. He pointed his flashlight toward the window of the haunted room. Maxwell followed but was having trouble keeping his balance as the tree swayed despite his physical strength and was pale and trembling.

"Look there," Alexander pointed to a place in the tree

that seemed stable. "We could bring a ladder from the basement, put it in the tree between these branches and climb up to the window. Do you agree?" he continued, but Maxwell was so nervous he didn't hear him.

"OK, let's go to bed and we'll do it after school tomorrow," Alexander suggested.

"No, No," Maxwell interrupted, "let's do it now. We should wait here until the ghost comes - if he really exists," he whispered, "Let's do it now," he insisted, clearly shaken, trying to convince himself that the ghost didn't exist. In either case, he wanted proof!

Alexander was tired and would have preferred to wait, but Maxwell insisted that they stay. Alexander's Mother was already asleep as her TV roared on. He didn't have to worry about waking her. He hoped she didn't wake up; she wouldn't like what they were doing.

The two explorers snuck downstairs, opened the door to the secret chamber, got the ladder and a lasso type of rope to tie the ladder on to the tree. They stood it against the big tree. Alexander climbed up with the lasso, threw it around a few branches and Maxwell attached it to the ladder. He grabbed the rope with both hands and pulled it up into the tree as Alexander guided it into a secure place between the branches. The ladder reached just under William McCoy's haunted chamber. Alexander did most of the work; Maxwell was too nervous. He held the flashlight with his hands shaking, to give Alexander lots of light. Then they both climbed back into Alexander's room.

"We need to secure both of us with a belt so we don't slip off the ladder, but I don't know if we should tie it to the front or back of the belt." Explained Alexander. So he went to his computer to look it up. "You can die if you fall from that height," he mumbled.

This made Maxwell more anxious. Alexander went on the web and searched on 'mountain climbing'. He found that the security rope should be attached to the back of the belt otherwise the jolt from a fall could break a climber's back and paralyze him. As he searched, Maxwell paced the room and Pluto followed each boy, wondering what they were doing. He looked perplexed.

Exhausted, the boys laid down on Alexander's bed and immediately fell asleep.

*   *   *

They were in a deep sleep when the old Grandfather clock rang twelve times announcing midnight, and when the ringing ended there was loud knocking followed by a man's scream: "Help me, help me, let me out, help me!!!" followed by footsteps and more violent knocking that made the room vibrate. Maxwell woke from his sleep and felt like he was hit by lightening. He jolted up and bolted around the room.

"What is that?" he yelled and grabbed Alexander to wake him. The knocking, banging and screaming continued: "Help me, help me, somebody help me!!!" Maxwell got back into bed and pulled the blanket over his head. He was scared but Alexander didn't wake up.

Finally, Alexander woke up, sat up and asked, "What's the problem?" The knocking, screaming and banging got worse.

"Can't you hear the screams, - it - it must be a real person, not a ghost!" Maxwell stuttered, trembling with fear when more screams were heard... "Help me, help me!!!"

"Mom, mom!" Maxwell cried and shook like a leaf. He was as white as a sheet and pulled the blanket tighter around his head and his body except for his right eye, in case he'd see something. He kept moving closer to Alexander, who kept his cool and tried to calm Maxwell.

"Don't worry, he'll go soon." But, Maxwell, the strong super-stud, was destroyed by fear. Nothing helped. Alexander took his friend by the shoulder and hugged him.

Maxwell was shivering. More knocking, more loud screams, heavy footsteps sounded like the ghost was breaking through the ceiling. If he did, he would attack them... so he continued to hide under the covers. Suddenly came, BOOM! BANG! CRACK! a sound so loud the wooden house almost exploded. Maxwell saw a larger than life figure towering above him. The ghost was flying covered by a white sheet. He could see scary eyes and teeth as white as snow... and then the screaming again, "Help, Help, Help ME!!!" so loud it almost broke Maxwell's eardrums. The yelling was followed by more yelling. Maxwell was ready to pass out, but Alexander stayed calm and was still half asleep.

Maxwell was now in tears; afraid he would wet his pants. He jumped out of bed and crawled under it in a fetal position. Pluto climbed in beside him licking his face, hoping to pacify and calm him. "Mom, help, help me!!" Maxwell whimpered. Alexander knew that the noise would soon be over and slipped back into dreamland. Shortly after, Maxwell put his arm out from under the bed and shook him gently. The noise had subsided, and he poked his head out from under the bed. "Alexander is it safe?" he whispered. Alexander came out of his dreamland and looked down at him. "Yes," he assured him. "Are you ready to explore?"

"No - No, not tonight." He was still shaking and was as pale as a ghost. Alexander smiled and was glad that he now had a witness that the ghost was real. Maxwell, still shaking, wiggled back under the bed and slept there the rest of the night next to Pluto. That was the last time Maxwell asked to sleep over.

The next morning the two boys made a gentlemen's agreement that they would never again speak about that night. And they never did.

*   *   *

A few days later Alexander was sitting on the stairs outside Professor Finley's classroom preparing for the lesson. Professor Finley had been strange during the last class and the students were more baffled about his behavior than they usually were.

Alexander and the others entered the room and sat at their desks. They were unusually quiet and well-behaved. Professor Finley rushed into the classroom, went to the blackboard, grabbed a piece of chalk and wrote on it so violently that the chalk splintered, as he waved his paralyzed arm in circles. He wrote: WEAPONS OF MASS DESTRUCTION. He swiftly turned toward the class and rambled on. "The Nuclear Bomb is powerful, but it will not obliterate our universe. The H-bomb, the Hydrogen Bomb, is much more destructive. The difference is whether it is a fusion weapon or a fission weapon, the H-bomb is a fusion weapon and the most powerful we have ever known," he paused with a wild look. "One day one of you, - oh – eh - one of us," he corrected himself, "will develop a weapon so powerful that it will destroy our planet, - a Matter--Anti-Matter weapon. An Anti-Matter bomb does not only exist in theory, but several brilliant scientists are, right now, developing such a weapon. These are people I know and one day you will meet. They have made great strides to solve the anti-matter puzzle. They will, maybe with your help, *develop this powerful tool. They will control the world and THEY will be the new leaders of the universe.*" His glare excited the students. Alexander was sure that Professor Finley was deliberately avoiding eye contact with him.

"The Anti-Matter Bomb will make the fusion nuclear bomb look like a firecracker!" Professor Finley rattled on with white foam forming around his mouth. He lectured on as if he had personally developed this weapon. Most of the students looked confused; it was over their heads. Except Alexander, who saw it as a message for him. But why was Professor Finley revealing this information to the whole class, and was he giving the same lecture to his other classes?

*   *   *

After the class Alexander went to sit on the staircase and search his computer, trying to find out if Professor Finley had ever published anything about Anti-Matter weapons, or why he seemed so preoccupied with the Anti-Matter issue. Then Maxwell came rushing by.

"Hi Alexander, are you all right?" he expressed, as he rushed back upstairs to the class.

He stopped and they talked for a few minutes. Maxwell had forgotten his cell-phone, but had now got it and was in a good mood.

"Hey Dude…" Alexander said, "do you want to come to my house to work out and check out Mr. McCoy's secret chamber? The ladder is still tied to the tree."

"Yes, let's do it today," Maxwell answered. A few hours later they were on their way to Alexander's house. As soon as they got off the bus, Maxwell walked ahead, his head held high, feeling very brave. Alexander tried to keep up but was struggling with a very heavy backpack. He always brought home too many books and his old computer was also heavy -- but he wanted to be well prepared for classes.

Maxwell's backpack was much lighter. Why should he bring books home when he knew his pal Alexander did? They saw Pluto and heard his welcoming bark.

The boys went to the kitchen and found a few open-faced sandwiches that Mary King had made for them. His mom had cautioned them about eating too much carbohydrate. Two pieces of bread was a lot, but only one slice of bread was better, and it was good to see what you were eating.

After they finished their snack, they put on their explorer outfits and went out to check on the ladder. They needed more rope and another security belt, so they went down to the basement to get them and at the same time grabbed two powerful flashlights. Alexander also stuck a knife into his belt.

They tied the security belt around Maxwell and attached a lasso to the back of the belt. They were both excited but suddenly Maxwell started to get nervous. A few minutes earlier he had such confidence and now he was looking scared. He had heard the angry ghost's scream and he knew what to expect.

Alexander noticed his reluctance, and that he was stalling by asking questions like, "Is the rope strong enough?" "Is the ladder safe?" "Are you coming with me?"

Hesitating, Maxwell said, "Maybe -- maybe, I should stay down here and hold the ladder for you."

"Nah," responded Alexander. "I want you to see William McCoy."

"Of course," Maxwell stuttered.

Alexander grabbed the end of the rope, attached it to the back of Maxwell's security belt and started to climb, followed by Maxwell. As they climbed, they twisted the security rope around a tree branch so that it would hold Maxwell's weight in case he slipped. Alexander held the end of the rope. They moved up. The window to the secret chamber was dangerously dark and creepy this afternoon.

"Be brave, there's nothing to worry about," Alexander reassured Maxwell who still looked scared. Little by little Alexander loosened the security rope that he held firmly to make sure Maxwell was able to move higher and higher.

A powerful gust of wind hit the tree and slammed it against the house. Maxwell grabbed the ladder firmly with both hands and quickly moved back down a few steps. Alexander urged him to go back.

"Don't worry, keep going," his voice could barely be heard above the sound of the wind. Maxwell was shaking but he continued to go up, pulling himself to the top, holding onto the ladder with one hand and grabbing the windowsill with the other. He pulled himself up, resting his face against the window as he tried to look inside. The room was pitch black as he scanned it, then he saw something move. "Oh my God," he whispered to himself, as he drew back and looked away.

"Is everything okay?" yelled Alexander, against the loud wind.

Maxwell didn't dare speak. He was sure that it was William McCoy who was inside and worried about being seen. He collected himself and held up his flashlight. He was shaking so hard that he had trouble turning it on. When he had calmed down, he moved back towards the window and aimed his flashlight into the dark room. The reflection was blinding. He closed his eyes for a second and looked again. When he opened his eyes, he heard a loud cracking noise and a movement right in front of the window.

Like lightning, a black shadow was in front of his face. "Dong! Bum! Bang!" came the sound.

Maxwell screamed, "WO-ow, hoo-ey!!!!" dropped the flashlight, pushed the ladder away from the house and fell screaming. Alexander almost lost his grip on the security rope, but regained his composure, and pulling hard on the rope, was able to stop Maxwell's free fall. He heard the "Bum! Bum!" as the flashlight hit the tree branches as it fell to the ground. But he held the rope.

Maxwell banged his right leg against the ladder and the branches during his fall, but the security rope attached to his back saved him from falling and hurting himself more, perhaps even dying. He dangled in the air with his legs and arms kicking the air. The tree branch to which the rope was attached was flexible and had minimized the force of the fall. Maxwell was still screaming as Alexander loosened the security rope and lowered him to the ground!

Alexander cut him free of the rope and they went to the kitchen to get an ice pack for his bruised leg. They then went out to move the ladder and take all the equipment back to the basement. He had to erase all signs of their activity. He noticed a mysterious hole in one of the glass panels to the secret chamber, but he didn't find any glass pieces or other signs of a broken window! A mystery... Maxwell was sure that the ghost had punched him through the window.

Alexander looked up at window and wondered what really happened. Did the ghost punch Maxwell in the face or did something fly out through the window? He went back to Maxwell, who was still shaken. He looked at Alexander and whispered, "Alexander, what was that?"

"I don't know, and we might never know. But I do know that this house is haunted." They were silent and they knew they would never talk about what happened that day.

*   *   *

Alexander the Great's Glasses

Alexander was now very happy with his life. He had good friends and he trained hard in his Martial Art classes. He was growing physically. He was very good at defending himself and was winning competitions. His mental acumen was building as was his confidence. He was following Dr. Schaller's nutritional plan, but he was still smaller than Maxwell or Gregory, who were a year older, and he had time to catch up.

When alone at home he would go down to his secret chamber and continue to look through his dad's things looking for clues as to his whereabouts. He checked everything. He got excited one time when he found his dad's Martial Arts box. It had his dad's uniform with his initials and some pamphlets. There was also a box that had his dad's Black Belt. Now he understood why Master Toku spoke so admiringly about his dad, and he missed him more. And he had a reason to learn Greek so he could read more of his dad's secret book.

He was even more motivated to work hard in Master Toku's classes. He was winning competitions and testing well enough to earn a White Belt. He was exceptionally good at the kicking exercises and sometimes he felt he possessed extraordinary strength. He was short, but fast and flexible. He could reach his competitors head with his feet even if they were much taller. He learned to kick, maintain his balance, twist up to four times and kick. Alexander felt like an ice skater who could successfully make triple and even quadruple jumps, turn in the air, land on their feet on slippery ice. He practiced harder than anyone in his class. Maxwell and Gregory, his seniors, often came over to encourage him and give him tips, which added to making him the best in his league. He excelled and was awarded a Yellow Belt. He was so good he earned his Green Belt soon after.

*   *   *

Every opportunity he had he would search through his dad's things. He found more uniforms and military equipment. He found booklets on how to change identities, how to avoid falling into the enemy's hands, and to never reveal one's name or military rank to the enemy. There were booklets demonstrating what happened to people who were caught snitching and how to identify people who lied to save themselves. He found fascinating material on what to do when captured by the enemy and how to run counterintelligence. He learned how to pick locks and could now open any of the locked boxes he found. He also found classified documents and videos made by his dad. He studied these documents and played the videos on an old VCR he found. He now knew so much more about his dad.

He had watched a video of his dad talking about how to penetrate the enemy line using various camouflage as well as an advanced jiu-jitsu technique and was in great spirit at dinner, just before his mom took him to Karate class. He very much wanted to tell his mom about his discoveries and the secret basement rooms.

The candlelight gave off a peaceful glow in the dining room as they sat at the round table. "You look more and more like your dad" his mother said, breaking the silence and giving Alexander the opening to tell her of his findings, but one thing led to another and they had to hurry to get to class in time. His mom was a good driver and she enjoyed driving the Volvo her husband had bought for her. At the time, he said that it was the safest car around, and would provide protection in case of an accident.

Alexander wanted to tell his mom that he had found so many of his dad's things and that he really missed him. Suddenly he grabbed her arm, "Careful, the traffic is terrible," she called out as she held tighter on the steering wheel.

"I know," he responded, "I want to tell you something."

"What is it? she replied as she quickly glanced at him.

"Mom you told me never to lie," he continued.

"Yes, one must always tell the truth."

"I know," he nodded. Then a few minutes passed where neither of them talked. Mary King was concentrating on driving and Alexander was thinking about how to tell her what was on his mind. Then the light of a car crossing in front of them almost blinded him. This made him speak.

"Well," he confessed as he looked at his mother, "I did not really lie -- there was just something I never told you." She again glanced at him, as if she was wondering what he was talking about.

"Well," he went on as he looked right at her, "I found, I mean we found, the secret door to daddy's basement chamber."

"You what?" his Mother snapped.

"I found the way to get downstairs and I have been looking through daddy's belongings," he continued before his mom had a chance to respond, "I have played with daddy's military outfits and worked out in his gym." He continued to look at her, "Both Maxwell and Gregory have seen it and we all are working out in the gym. I am sorry mom, but I feel very close to daddy when I go downstairs!" His Mother was about to say something, but he was so worried he continued talking.

"Mom I did not know dad had a Black Belt? Now I understand why Master Toku was so impressed with him when we first met."

"Yes, your dad is an amazing man and he is still alive - I feel it in my soul!" she responded, almost crying, "He loves you so much," she wiped tears and continued, "and I also miss him. It is all so wrong, but I know he will be back!" She had slowed down so as not to have an accident. They were both silent for a while. Alexander wondered if she was mad at him, and asked, "Mom, are you angry - I'm sorry."

"Sorry for what?" she responded.

"That we went downstairs," he answered.

"Ah, Alexander, of course not, it is our home - you can go anywhere. Just be careful and never play with fire. The house is made of wood and could easily burn," she lectured him calmly. Alexander smiled and was very relieved when they arrived for Master Toku's class.

*   *   *

He had grown closer to Gregory and Maxwell, but they were not real buddies. It was not like a relationship with a brother or a very close friend with whom one can discuss any small thing on one's mind. Alexander buried his sorrows by working and studying very hard. He liked to help Gregory and Maxwell with their homework, and he worshipped their friendship however close it was. They both liked Alexander and loved to go to his gym once or twice a week if they did not have soccer, tennis, soft ball or basketball practice. They were, unlike Alexander, very popular with girls and great in sports, but had no time for girls really. They liked girl fans – cheerleaders - and they accepted Christiana and Rebekah because they were so smart and helped them with their homework too. The girls wanted to do everything the cousins were doing. Rebekah had the hots for Maxwell and had decided that the only way to get closer to him was through Alexander. She was therefore beginning to move her chair right next to Alexander's whenever the professors were not in the classroom. After all Alexander was sitting in front of

Maxwell and she could easily turn and socialize with him.

One day when the professor was late and most of the kids loud and noisy, Rebekah was sitting at Alexander's table while he was helping Gregory with his test. Maxwell was talking soccer with another boy, and Rebekah was trying to get their attention.

"Hey!" Rebekah shouted, "are you guys going to Alexander's house today?"

"Yep," Gregory responded.

"Can I go with you?" she asked, "I hear the gym is very cool and I would love to work out with three pros."

"Yes," responded Gregory, it is a real hot gym. It has bikes, treadmills, and all kinds of weight-lifting equipment, ropes, and barbells, but it is not for girls. It will be too tough for you!"

"You do not want to be there, believe you me," Maxwell said with a smirking grin.

"Yes, I do," she answered back.

Rebekah quickly turned toward Alexander, touched his arm and begged, "Can I go with the three of you to your house today Alexander, please?"

Surprised and completely off-balance he almost stuttered, "Ye - - Yeah. If it is okay with your mom," he answered.

Rebekah was a real tomboy, growing up with her three older brothers. She was afraid of nothing and her father loved her; she could do nothing wrong. A few hours later she was on the bus with the boys on their way. Bob the bus driver smiled in approval.

Rebekah was euphoric as she ran toward the house. "Wow, what a great house," she called to Alexander, "I have seen it from the road but never been here."

They wind picked up and powerful trees were bending majestically, leaves were tinkling like bells as if welcoming the four musketeers. Pluto was barking and happy to see them all. Rebekah looked up just before she entered the house. She then realized how tall Alexander's 'golden mansion' was; it appeared as if it reached all the way up in the sky trying to kiss the clouds.

They went straight to the refrigerator and fetched the delicious open sandwiches and milk his mother had left. They soon climbed down to their underground world. The explorers had by now fixed all the lights and Maxwell turned them on as if this place was his home. Alexander was the quiet one; he was the nerdy type and did not talk much. But he was a time bomb -- he was strong and fast when he needed to be.

"What is that," Rebekah asked as she pointed to black area in an unlit corner of one of the adjacent rooms.

"Well, behind all these boxes is a big door that leads to a system of tunnels that run all the way up to the mountain and down to Forrestville," Gregory smiled. "If you don't behave, we'll lock you up down there to fight the wizards, trolls, snakes, lizards and all the creepy animals. The beasts would love to eat you up," he grinned.

"Oh! Stop it!" Rebekah jeered back and with her elbow hit him hard right in the stomach, so hard he doubled over in pain. "You are probably more scared than me," she laughed. Maxwell and Alexander just smiled. By then they had changed into their gym clothes and went into the gymnasium to start their workout. Rebekah thought the gym was cool. She began working out with ropes and medical balls, while the boys used the machines and the weight bars.

When Pluto later alerted them that Mary King was arriving, they slowly changed to their street clothes and went up to welcome Alexander's mom. They no longer needed to hide what they were doing but it was a habit. Rebekah's dad's driver, Edward, picked up the kids and took them home. This routine continued like clockwork from that day on.

*   *   *

Alexander jolted up in the middle of the night. In his dream he could hear a scream for help: "help, help, help me, help, help!" Was it his dad's voice? He ran to the window and opened it to look out. No screaming from outside. He waited a while, but since there was no more screaming, he went back to bed. His dreams had become much more vivid and who knows who would send messages for help. It frustrated him. He ruled out the ghost McCoy. This cry for help was entirely different.

That afternoon, searching through his dad's stuff

became more intense. He found pictures of his father and many secret codes he couldn't break. Then suddenly he came across an antique wooden eyeglass box that was wrapped in blue paper. He carefully opened it and a found a pair of antique squared rectangular glasses with a metal frame and temples. He polished them with a napkin and tried them on.

"Wow!" he exclaimed, "they fit perfectly!" He found several old fragile newspaper pages written in a foreign language with different characters than our alphabet. The newspaper wrapped the glasses. It seemed that the glasses had his correct sight adjustments so he could make out every letter, every word, in the old newspaper. It appeared to be Russian, but he couldn't be sure.

Awesome, he thought to himself. He kept the eyeglasses on and walked around. He checked himself out in a mirror and jumped in the air he was so pumped. He couldn't believe it. It was as if these glasses were made for him. Not only could he see razor sharply, he had a new look and he liked it. He jumped again and again in happiness, flexing his arms, biking his legs, and doing Karate moves. He had arrived!

Under the light Alexander realized that the metal frame and arms were golden, maybe made from real gold, he thought to himself. He re-examined the spectacles several times and realized that when he opened the arms of the glasses, small lateral mirrors opened up on each side of the rectangular frame. It looked as if the tiny mirrors were a part of the lateral vertical bars of the square golden frames. Wow - he could actually see behind himself. They were real 'spy glasses' with 360-degree surround vision, he confirmed. He examined the wooden box; it was old, handcrafted. He saw writings inside the box, but could not read it, although he thought it was in Russian from his knowledge of the letters, and it was similar to the newspaper wrap.

When Pluto alerted him, his mom was arriving he rushed upstairs, but almost forgot to change back to his old ugly oversized horn-rimmed eyeglasses. He told his Mother about his discovery and showed her the box wrapped in blue paper underneath the newspaper. He unpacked them carefully in front of her. "Mom they fit me," he said enthusiastically. He was frightened she would tell him to put them back. He looked nervously at her holding the spectacles in his hands.

"Your dad bought these golden glasses in St. Petersburg on one of his many trips," she smiled. "They were the personal belonging of the Great Russian Czar, Alexander II," she continued. Wow! Alexander was even more excited.

"Can I use the glasses mom?" he asked as he took off his large ugly horn-rimmed glasses with his left hand and slipped on his new golden rectangular amazing glasses with his right hand, with a big grin.

"Yes of course you can," she answered happily as she grabbed his old glasses and put them aside forever. "Your dad bought them for you to use when you got old enough, and I totally forgot about these remarkable golden beauties."

"Did you see the mirrors?" Alexander asked his mom as he pointed to the tiny mirrors on the lateral vertical bars. She nodded almost crying out of happiness for Alexander and sorrow for her husband. "The Czar Alexander must have been a smart man," Alexander commented. "Yes, he was a remarkable man, but he had many enemies. He had these spy glasses made to make sure he was safe from an attack from behind" his Mother explained. "They now belong to you, my own Alexander the Great," she smiled.

Alexander went on the computer that evening to find more information about the Great Czar Alexander II. He learned that he was a much-loved Czar and leader, known as the 'Good Czar,' and ruled Russia from 1855 to 1881. He promoted education and economic growth in the country and freed the serfs who were like slaves.

Sadly, like Abraham Lincoln, who also was a great president and freed the slaves in the US, he also created enemies. The Great Czar Alexander II was attacked by terrorists soon after he freed the serfs in Russia. President Lincoln was shot in a theater in Washington, DC in 1865, by actor John W. Booth.

When the Great Czar Alexander II drove through St. Petersburg on his way to a military roll call ceremony on Sunday March 13, 1881, a reactionary terrorist threw a bomb under his carriage. Many were killed but the Czar was unhurt, because he rode in a bulletproof carriage, a gift from Napoleon III of France.

Unfortunately, against military advice, the Good Czar stayed on the street to survey the damage and help others, and to try to find out who had performed such an atrocious attack, but moments later a second bomb was tossed by another reactionary terrorist. This one blew off his legs and killed him!

*   *   *

The spyglasses were very becoming for Alexander's face. He looked like a different person, and at once became more attractive with his brown curly hair and his unique glasses. He gained more self-confidence, and everyone liked his new look. Christi and Rebekah especially loved his 'Alexander the Great' glasses.

Mister Z.

A giant curtain of black clouds covered the sky and the classroom went pitch black. This happened precisely at the moment Professor Finley was hammering Alexander with questions. The classroom was so black that the kids couldn't see their noses. The blackening of the sky occurred so quickly and unexpectedly that even Professor Finley's voice cracked in surprise, but he continued his lecture and only his thick, rasping Irish accent indicated his whereabouts.

In vain, they searched for the light switches as the bell rang its song of freedom before the end of the class, and the lights came back on. The Headmaster saw that a major thunderstorm was moving towards Forrestville, and as he wouldn't risk anyone getting hurt, he decided to end the school day early.

Professor Finley's science class began before the blackout turned the mood of the class tense. He was targeting several kids, but especially Alexander. He had been hammering them with questions so difficult that no one could answer correctly, then turned on Alexander with a wicked look and called on him, "Maybe the little King can answer me?"

And, he got it right... every time.

That didn't stop or even slow him down. Just before the classroom went black, he had proclaimed, "Can our curly top dwarf answer me?" and of course, again Alexander got all the answers right, which was met by more anger from Professor Finley. That's when the blackout happened, almost as if it was a warning to him.

When the bell sounded, kids jumped up and ran out of the classrooms into the hallways. Most of them stayed there throughout the storm, but a few were stupid enough to run into the yard during the height of the thunder, lightning and torrential downpour. The five musketeers, as Alexander, Christi, Gregory, Maxwell and Rebekah now called themselves, found a corner in the hallway to talk about Professor Finley's maliciousness.

The evil trio: Christian 'The Snake' Chung, Devlin 'The Rat' Ratner, and Cain 'The Nose' Cavoli, decided to show what daredevils they were, and ran through the downpour only to return dripping like buckets of water. They were soaking wet and cold as they pushed the kids out of the way and ran up the stairs towards the 'five musketeers'.

Alexander's back was to them when he saw, in the mirrored frame of his surround glasses, Chris the 'Snake' with a bucket of water moving toward them. His four friends, now standing right outside the classroom door, did not see the danger. Alexander knew he had to stop him before he soaked them all. He continued to observe the 'Snake's' moves in his 'Alexander the Great' glasses and at the moment the 'Snake' lifted the bucket of water to throw it, Alexander pushed his friends out of the way and jumped. They tumbled to the side and the water missed them. The bucket flew out towards the classroom door just as Professor Finley exited the classroom, hitting him and soaking him down to his underwear. Without a doubt Professor Finley saw Christian Chung throw the bucket but turned on Alexander.

"You little devil," he screamed. "I want to see you after next class!"

"Wait a minute, Professor Finley," Rebekah and Christiana called out in unison. "We saw what happened and it wasn't Mr. King who threw the water; it was Mr. Chung." They paused, "And there are many witnesses."

Professor Finley sneered, turned on his heels, and ran down the hall to the teachers' lounge to change his wet clothes. Alexander was never called into Professor Finley's class, but neither was the Snake!

"Something is wrong here," said Gregory later, "why does he always favor the bad guys?"

"Yes, it is strange," replied Rebekah, "there's some sort of conspiracy going on here."

She paused; she had an idea. "I want you to come with me to see Mr. Zimmerman, my daddy's partner and friend. He's known as the 'wizard Mr. Z'. We'll go to see him before we go to Alexander's house this afternoon." She continued to rave about him, "He's a fantastic inventor and problem-solver, and may be able to help us with the Professor Finley mystery."

*　　*　　*

After school, Rebekah's father's driver and friend,

Edward, picked them up. The car weaved its way downhill on a long twisting slide into the valley and passed through curved roads and alleys lined with thousands of tall trees. It was a picturesque ride. Mr. Z lived in the valley on the outskirts of Forrestville beside a rolling river. He had bought a crumbling farm from an old widow who had gone bankrupt, but had allowed her to stay in her home on the ranch.

"So, who is this mystical Mr. Z?" Maxwell asked Rebekah.

"He's amazing. A researcher, a mad scientist and an inventor who together with my dad has patented hundreds of inventions. He developed oil drilling tools that have revolutionized my dad's oil exploration methods and helped him discover oil where no one even considered it a possibility. He has developed talking robots, an invisible barcode that alerts stores to attempted thefts and so much more," she said proudly. "Mr. Z studied computer science and electrical engineering in Munich, Germany, but dropped out when he realized he knew more than the professors."

"After he settled here, he met my dad and they partnered on many of these discoveries," she continued, "He created a labyrinth of laboratories along the stream using several large trailers that my dad helped him find, and my dad helped him build a waterpower station and put solar panels on the roofs of these trailers, that made him totally energy independent. You'll all be amazed."

Just then Edward crossed the water stream and drove

through a curved road up to farmhouse that was lined with Mr. Z's labyrinth of laboratories.

As soon as they drove up in front of Mr. Z's world of trailers, they were met by his two large Labradors, a yellow and a black. They barked violently and blocked the road, so Edward had to stop the car.

A woman ran out to greet them.

"Hi, Rebekah! He is waiting for you."

"Who is she?" whispered Gregory so the woman couldn't hear him.

"His wife," smiled Rebekah, "sort of!" she whispered as the woman poked her head through the window to greet her. They jumped out and ran over to the laboratories.

When Rebekah opened the side door into the trailer they were met with an awesome world of dense vegetation: plants, flowers and trees. It was an elaborate greenhouse.

"Mr. Z must be from outer space," said Alexander in awe, "I have never seen flowers and plants as big and as amazing as these."

"You're right," echoed Gregory, "this place is like a new biosphere."

"Just wait until you meet Mr. Z," said Rebekah as they continued on the twisted path, "you'll definitely think he's not from this world."

*　　*　　*

The vegetation become more and more dense, and

soon they were in an oasis of flowers and trees. They had this wonderful feeling of being in a garden of paradise. A little exotic bird flew between Rebekah and Alexander, followed by more colorful birds and creatures. There was a lot of humming and the swishing of flight.

"What is that?" wondered Gregory, as he looked at a tiny bird with a long bill that stopped in midair in front of him then flew backwards, staring at him.

"Hummingbirds," exclaimed Alexander, "the smallest and fastest bird on earth. A very intelligent and beautiful bird with a long bill to help it extract honey from flowers and catch insects."

"Yes," confirmed Rebekah, "Mr. Z breeds hummingbirds because they are such a fascinating species. He's studying their wings because of their ability to fly forward, backward, and up and down. The secret to their flight helps us understand how to propel helicopters and similar equipment, he told my dad."

*   *   *

The path suddenly became dark as they reached the end of the jungle of trailers. They didn't see a door to the laboratory, but they did see layers of heavy rubber-like panels hanging from the ceiling. They were there to keep the hummingbirds safely inside. The place was intricately sealed while people passed through.

Maxwell tumbled through the rubber door panels, and the lane curled into a well-lit room.

He hesitated as Rebekah pushed him forward and told him to go faster. He was annoyed and turning back, yelled, "Get off me."

He turned and was frightened by a large uniformed man who popped up in front of the group unexpectedly and yelled, "STOP!"

"Uhh, ahh, ahh," Maxwell cried and bolted backward nearly falling. Not looking where he was going he pushed Rebekah and Gregory to the side and started running with hands above his head. Both Maxwell and Gregory were so shaken they forgot they were martial arts experts. Rebekah, froze but wasn't frightened by the man.

Alexander stayed calm and stood staring fearlessly at the man.

"Stop - stop you all... Show me IDs," the man called out to them.

"We're friends of Mister Z," said Rebekah with authority.

The room was silent except for Maxwell's moan, and the man looked at them with curiousity. They realized that the man was listening to a message coming through his earphone. His face relaxed and he bowed, saluted, and signaled for them to come with him.

They moved through another door and the laboratory came alive. There were robots shuffling around, and flying monster-like creatures leaping over their heads, talking, counting and laughing. It was a circus of human-like robots. Mini robots were frolicking on the side shelves. Cavorting, jumping up and down and calling out to the 'musketeers' as they passed by them. They appeared to be little people; some would jump up toward the ceiling, grab a trapeze and swing back to their station. They were entertaining. They laughed and played.

A green Quaker Parrot was swinging on a trapeze bar and when Maxwell passed, the parrot screamed, 'STOP! – POLICE! – STOP!' then laughed. Then a beautiful Grey African Parrot robot echoed the words as the group cautiously walked past. It was an awesome labyrinth and an amazing experience.

As they moved through the 'robot world' they found a team of mini-robots playing soccer. The soccer field was about three to four feet long and two to three feet wide. It sat on a shelf, and you could see it from all sides. It held two teams of twelve miniature robot players. It looked like it was motion activated and the game was actually activated when someone came close to it.

"Awesome, eh!" called Maxwell, who saw how well they played. And as an expert player he knew when the game was going well.

"We could improve our game if we had a set like this," he said enthusiastically.

As they moved through they came to a motion activated electric train, which was puffing through mountain terrain, lined with waterfalls and trees. The train climbed to the top of the mountain and stopped at a station where some mini-robots got off. The train and the station seemed so real that as you walked beside it, you felt like you were riding by it. The rail tracks twisted through scenic terrain and the train moved through a tunnel and over a miniature bridge. It was all so real; there were cows and horses moving over the land and none collided. Alexander was fascinated with the electric train set. He loved trains. He found these more awesome than anything he'd seen before. They finally reached the end of the robot world as a group of small robots danced, laughed and clapped as they walked through the door and found themselves in a laboratory.

It was full of machines, computers, and wired workstations. There were hundreds of mysterious drawings on the walls. Gregory, who was leading the group, was the first to notice a couple of men working on a large robot. The older man was attaching wires to the robot's body and the younger one was lying on the floor attaching a part to its lower body. Gregory pointed to the older man and whispered to Rebekah, "Hey, is that Mr. Z?"

"No," laughed Rebekah, "that's not Mr. Z."

The kids
moved through
the wizard's
laboratory
which was
alive with
noisy
machines, and
moved past
them. They
walked
gingerly afraid
to set off a land
mine or disrupt
this amazing
place. They
then went into
a small room

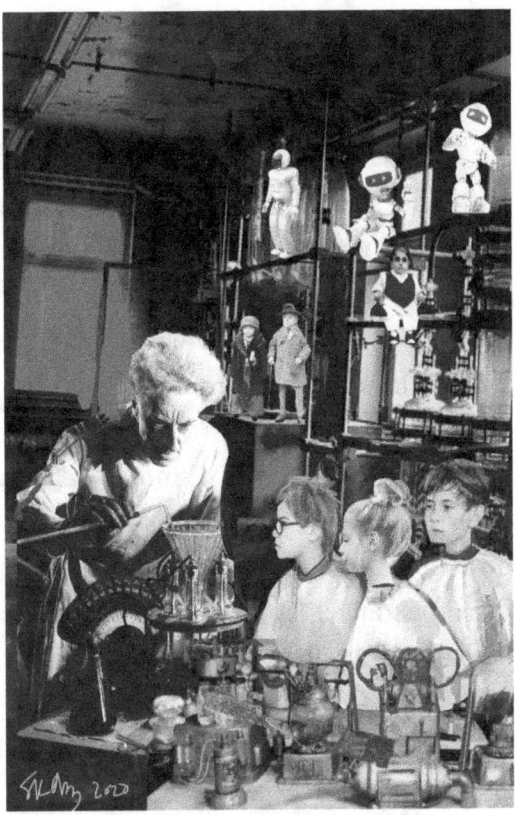

where two young people were working at a large
computer terminal.

At the next laboratory, they were stunned by all the
gizmos and animal-like creatures stacked on shelves.
There was everything from spy stuff to clothes, shoes
and even a miniature racing car. Rebekah stopped and
explained that one of Mr. Z's inventions was a computer
system that linked up retail stores' information and
inventory. If someone bought a bar of soap, the
computer would register the sale and immediately
replace it, giving the store manager total control. It

registered the payment, so if someone took it without paying, the bar code would trigger an alarm as they left the store.

Rebekah, who referred to Mr. Z as her uncle, was searching the cubicle looking for him, and finally found him in a sealed laboratory wing lying on the floor attaching tubes and cylinders to a 'Frankenstein-type' machine. Mr. Z rose slowly to his feet but continued to check the wires until he was sure that they were in the right place. He was a tall lean man with long fuzzy white hair and a nicely trimmed beard, and was wearing a large lab coat with tools sticking out of several of its pockets. Alexander fixated on his unique sneakers and his appearance. He looked so much like Albert Einstein, Alexander thought, old but ageless. Alexander liked him.

"Hi uncle, what are you up to?" called Rebekah and ran to hug him.

"Fixing an old wizard," he laughed.

"So what's on your mind, friends?" he asked.

Rebekah introduced the boys to Mr. Z and they gave him their story about Professor Finley and his strange behavior.

"He's especially bad to Alexander," Rebekah said, "and we'd like to know why and what he is up to?"

"Finley, James Finley?!" Mr. Z mumbled to himself as he typed the name into his computer. "Oh yes," he exclaimed, "James Winston Finley... I know him. He tried to steal one of our patents. He's a bad man," Mr. Z said, and continued his search. "I have a picture of his house," pulling up a strange looking home on his large screen. "Yes, there's something rotten here," he looked worried.

Mr. Z asked them to leave and directed them from the laboratory complex through a back door. He guided them along the stream back to their car. "Don't worry," he assured the group,

"We'll get to the bottom of this." He grasped Alexander's shoulders and spoke directly to him. "Come back in a few days and we'll continue our investigation."

*   *   *

A few days later Rebekah went over to Alexander's table and pulled up a chair beside him.

"Mr. Z wants to see us," she whispered, "is today ok?"

"Cool," said Alexander.

"Great," she whispered back, "Maxwell and Gregory can't go, but I will see you at the parking lot after class!" Alexander was flattered that she wanted him to go with her.

After school they drove to Mr. Z's laboratory. When they arrived, the Labradors ran out to greet them, but they weren't there to block them from entering; they welcomed them, jumping up to lick their faces. Mr. Z's lady-friend told them to take the footpath alongside the labyrinth buildings and he would meet them at the end.

An unmarked door swung open with a loud bang.

Rebekah jumped and screamed. When she recovered, she saw the mighty Mr. Z at his private lab way at the end of the corridor. He signaled them to come in and they ran over to him.

Alexander was surprised to see how Mr Z looked compared to their last visit. At their last visit he wore a dirty old lab coat with tools and tubes sticking from its pockets. Today he was tall and fit, and was dressed in casually in worn, but well-fitting, blue jeans and a large T-shirt with a modified wide leather weightlifting belt on his hips. The belt was about 3 inches wide, and was secured with a large antique bronze buckle engraved with a large Z. There was also an eagle imprint on its sides. Awesome, Alexander thought, as he studied Mr. Z's sneakers' thick soles that made him look even taller. They looked like a mix of workout shoes and boxing boots that reached his ankles. They seemed sturdy and each was engraved with a Z.

"How are you my friends?" Mr. Z welcomed them.

"We're so excited to see you," Rebekah said hugging him.

"Hope we're not interrupting you," said Alexander.

"No, I just finished pumping iron, so this is a good time," Mr. Z explained.

Alexander was even more impressed with Mr. Z. He looked amazing; tall and wizard-looking with his long curly white hair and beard.

"Great belt! Cool." Alexander said.

"Thank you," he replied, "I made it myself. The eagles represent the 'Screaming Eagle' company I was part of in the military. Love eagles!" he smiled. "I wear this belt during my work outs. It gives good support and protection for my back."

He surprised Alexander when he asked, "Would you like me to make one for you?"

"Ye-Yeah," Alexander stuttered, "I would love one."

"Great," Mr. Z replied. "What's your favorite animal?"

"I - I love dogs, but my favorite animal is the bald eagle because it's the largest and smartest of all eagles. It's a powerful animal, a beautiful predator with a white feathered head. It kills rats, snakes and foxes - many of the animals that attack farmers' chickens and even house animals - and protect the land," he announced proudly.

"Bravo," said Mr. Z, "you certainly know your stuff."

"Do you want me to engrave a bald eagle on your belt?" asked Mr. Z.

"Well, not really," Alexander answered a bit uncomfortably. "I love the lion, the king of animals."

"Oh! And why is that?" asked Mr. Z, knowing that he'd get a good response from Alexander.

"Because his name is Alexander King," Rebekah giggled.

"No," Alexander snapped. "The lion is a majestic animal and the top predator. The male lion is a strong and proud animal. They protect their females and their cubs on their personal territory against other males who intrude on their territory. Like a king, they guard their subjects. A lion represents bravery, strength and pride. That's why it's considered the king of the jungle," Alexander said with a great deal of pride.

"A wonderful explanation," said Mr. Z, "so you want me to engrave a lion on your belt?"

"Yeah, I would love that."

"Done!" Mr. Z, pulled out a measuring tape and measured Alexander's waist and made notes.

"My favorite animal is the dolphin," Rebekah said, not wanting to be left out of this conversation. "I'm a water sign and love dolphins because they're very smart and enjoy human beings. They can scare sharks away and are loyal and mate for life, like mom and dad. We are like dolphins and we are devoted friends," she said, looking at Alexander. Alexander blushed.

"Well, let's get back to Professor Finley," Mr. Z brought them back to the purpose of their visits. He led them to a computer room where he pulled up an enlarged picture of Professor Finley's house.

"This is more like a fortress, than a home," suggested Mr. Z, "no ordinary teacher or professor can afford such a house. I sent some students over but it's well protected by a wired fence and attack dogs. They couldn't even get near the fence."

"He's up to something bad and must be getting big money from somewhere other than Forrestville

Academy," he went on. "It's definitely not just his home, but may have an underground complex," he squinted and furrowed his brows, "but that doesn't explain why he's so mean to you Alexander. But maybe he's looking for someone to take attention away from himself? He is definitely a dangerous person and we need to keep our eyes on him!"

"What can we do?" asked Rebekah.

"Well, I'll make a gadget that can be attached to Professor Finley's car so that I can track his movements on my own GPS monitors," Mr. Z explained. "I can have it ready in a few days. I'll send you a message to come back when it's ready." He smiled and said goodbye to them.

*   *   *

They got the message a week later and Rebekah, Maxwell and Alexander crawled into Edward's car and they drove the scenic route to this amazing man's laboratories. They were sitting quietly watching and enjoying the astonishing drive up the serpentine road when Rebekah excitingly broke the silence.

"My family is going to our Uthea Mountain Ranch for the school break in a couple of weeks and would like to invite you all to join us."

"Don't think I can go," as Maxwell counted the days on his fingers, "I'll have soccer training during that break," he said somewhat regrettably.

"You'll miss a trip of a lifetime," the driver, Edward

announced, "the Big Canyon Ranch is unreal," and he smiled.

"Yes it is," echoed Rebekah, "It's an awesome place and besides, school is closed and there won't be any sports training," she snapped.

"I – I would love to go if Maxwell can make it," Alexander was excited at the idea. He had looked up the place on his computer. It wasn't an ordinary ranch. It was an old European Castle that her great, great grandfather brought to America, stone by stone. He rebuilt it on his ranch in the Uthea Mountains to its original architectural glory and majesty. The photos showed a magnificent fortress. He would love to explore this sensational castle.

They were silent for the rest of the drive. The beauty of their surroundings was overwhelming. Maxwell looked confused.

"There it is," Alexander suddenly broke the silence and pointed to Mr. Z's estate.

They were again welcomed by the big dogs, followed by Mr. Z who came personally to greet them.

"Welcome back," the big, gentle scientist grinned. He was again dressed in blue jeans, large shirt with an eagle imprinted on its back, the shoes and his leader belt. He took them through the back door into a row of labs where several people were working, and into his office.

"Here it is," he said, and held up a device the size of a small cell phone. "It has to be attached to the Professor's car, either under the car seat or if you can't get in, under the chassis. It has a powerful magnet, and can be pushed up against the side or the back end of the car. But make sure it can't be seen."

The scientist looked at the kids and asked them if they understood his instructions.

"I can pick it up with my GPS, know where he is and what he's doing even when he's not in the car," he was very excited about the gadget's capabilities.

"I think we can do that," replied Rebekah and put the device in her bag. "Uncle, I forgot to tell you that I invited my friends to the Canyon Ranch in about two weeks," she announced cheerfully.

"Oh my, are you in for an amazing time," exclaimed Mr. Z, "Don't miss the chance to go. Glad I made the power belts in time for your trip," and gave Rebekah and Alexander their special leather power belts, which were similar to his own power belt.

"Wow, thank you – It's magnificent!" Alexander jumped in joy as he looked the belt over. The bronze buckle had a big A, and a brilliant lion was engraved on each side of the belt.

Mr. Z had created an amazing Coat d'Arms for Alexander. It was a stunning seal with lions on both sides of a golden globe around an 'A' surrounded by a colorful array of flags, two swords crossed and 'REX' written underneath. This same imprint was on the back of Alexander's awesome power belt. He was thrilled.

Rebekah's belt had a golden buckle with an 'R' and a

beautiful dolphin embedded on each side. Her emblem was the colorful Harkens Family Coat d'Arms that was visible all over the Academy.

"Do you want one as well, Maxwell?" Mr. Z asked.

"Yes, I would, thank you," he responded.

"What is your favored animal? "

"Well I love horses," he responded as Mr. Z started to measure his waist.

They were all excited and prepared to deal with Professor Finley.

*   *   *

They were busy with tests at school so had no time for anything else for a few days, but as soon as the exams were over, Rebekah joined the boys at their table.

"Let's meet in the staff parking lot after class," she whispered.

"Ok," responded Alexander. Maxwell agreed.

Maxwell got there first. He sat down on a bench and texted Rebekah and Alexander. They got there a few minutes later, and they walked around the lot checking if anyone was hanging out.

"Which one is his car?" asked Maxwell.

"It's a Mercedes Benz with darkened windows. There it is," Alexander pointed.

"Should we check if it's locked?" asked Rebekah.

"No, no way," said Alexander, "if his house is as wired as Mr. Z said, then surely his car will have the same security traps!"

"Give me the device," he whispered looking around, scanning the lot. Let's walk to the back of the car and, Rebekah, drop your bag. I'll bend to pick it up and attach the device under the car."

Rebekah handed Alexander the device. After studying it, he knew how to best place it and if he had room to push it in further. He had checked the Internet and had a good picture of this model of Mercedes Benz. They walked to the car observing their surroundings. Rebekah dropped her bag as instructed. Alexander kneeled down and pretending to pick it up, he pushed the device up behind the tire and heard the powerful magnet attach itself. It was well hidden. He picked up the bag and handed it to Rebekah, saying, "Rebekah, you dropped your bag." They laughed and headed to the school bus.

They were working out in Alexander's gym a few days later, when Alexander broached the question to Maxwell. "So, are we going to the Harkens Ranch?"

"Don't know yet," said Maxwell.

They continued to work out until they heard his mom coming into the house, and they quickly ran up to Alexander's room. Alexander sat down at the computer and pulled up the Harkens Uthea estate on his computer screen and showed it to Maxwell.

"I'd love to see this place," he said wistfully. "I've never really traveled so my mom is all for me going!"

"Yeh, my mom wants me to go too," nodded Maxwell, "but I don't think I can," he shrugged.

*　　*　　*

Maxwell maintained this position, and a few days later they were picked up by Mr. Z's driver and driven back to his magnificent laboratory. The trees along the way were inviting but the group wasn't very happy. Rebekah was annoyed with Maxwell, but she and Alexander talked casually about their upcoming trip.

When the car reached its destination, the Labradors came further down the road to welcome them. They surrounded the car, barking and jumping. The lovely lady came out to meet them and told them to go down to the last trailer where Mr. Z was waiting for them. They enjoyed their trip through the trailers where the robot soldiers entertained them as they walked through each trailer.

Mr. Z welcomed them with a big grin. "Got great tracking info on the devil professor," he enthused as he pulled up a map of Forrestville. "His movements reveal a lot of monkey business, He goes to the same places every day as if he was checking on something or someone. I should have more details soon," he sounded confident.

Mr. Z took Maxwell's belt from the shelf and gave it to him.

"You'll get a lot of use out of this and will help support your back on your hunting trips at the Uthea estate."

"Thank you, thank you!" Maxwell bowed.

"Max is not going," said Rebekah, sounding very

sad.

A surprised Mr. Z replied, "Well, maybe he has to work in his dad's chocolate stores," and as he smiled, Maxwell felt hypnotized and his face looked flushed. Mr. Z took a couple of wands off the shelf and handed them to Rebekah and Alexander. They were different colors.

"I want you to have these Power Batons. They're handcrafted. A push of this button," he pointed to a silver button, "turns it into a walking cane. When pressed again a large knife is ejected and it becomes a deadly weapon. This other button will turn the knife into a sword. I call it a 'Wunder Wand'. It will come in handy when you come across snakes or other creepies. It also has powerful built-in flashlight and an alarm." He demonstrated both as their eardrums were attacked by a loud scream. It was so loud and frightening that they had to cover their ears and close their eyes. "That was another feature. You can mimic animal screams. They help you scare off most of the predators you come across." He showed them how to attach the cane to their belts and loop it on their wrists. He nodded in satisfaction with his handywork.

He grabbed another Wunder Wand and handed it to Maxwell. "Just in case you decide to join them." Mr. Z smiled.

Then Mr. Z opened another cabinet, took out three packets each the size of a small handbag, and put them on the desk. He unfolded one and explained what was in it. "These knapsacks are for your excursion. They're made of a very strong but ultra thin and light material called graphene. It's not like your school knapsacks. It's light and includes a pair of flexible straps that wrap around the shoulders making it easier for long trips. There's also a tent made from the same graphene material. Folded, it's no bigger than your fist, but open, it can easily sleep two people." He pulled the string and threw it to an empty space, and bingo, it expanded into a two-man tent. The kids were amazed.

He gave one to each of them. A red one to Rebekah, a blue to Alexander and a green to Maxwell.

Next, Mr. Z gave each a baseball-style explorer cap that had an invisible net that folded over the ears, to guard them from mosquitoes and bees, both of which were common on the estate.

"I think you already have my special explorer boots?" he asked Rebekah.

"Yes Uncle, I'll bring them."

"Voila, here are your boots, Alexander!" Mr. Z announced, as he reached over to a shelf and handed him a pair of ankle boots similar to his own, with thick waterproofed outer soles that would also make Alexander taller. They were white, black and blue, with reflector stripes of orange, yellow and green in a stunning combination. The golden 'A' was engraved on each. "They are golden because you live on the golden hills," Mr. Z grinned, and continued to describe this item too, "There's a secret pocket inside the soles for money and keys." He opened a small lid inside the boots and showed him the hidden space.

"I covered the soles with a chemical that can be activated by pulling a string. It will produce enough gas to increase the sole thickness by two inches giving you extra height for fighting bigger enemies. These are *Power Boots,*" he said, as he pointed to the string.

"Wow, awesome!" and as he looked at Mr. Z, the man's eyes burrowed into his own with such force that Alexander felt himself trembling.

"Awesome," repeated Alexander still shaking. He had felt this same trembling before. Once when Dr. Schaller stared at him, and again with Professor Silversmith. Was it a message, he thought.

"Bon Voyage," smiled Mr. Z as they walked through the labyrinth to the car. Mr Z's driver drove them back to their respective homes.

The Big Canyon Ranch

The sun was raising its smiling face over the clear blue horizon on a glorious cloud-free morning. A few rays penetrated holes in the wooden shutters on Rebecca's windows sending bullets of sharp sunlight on to her face. She covered her eyes but soon began to awaken.

She jumped up realizing she needed to get ready to leave for the Uthea Mountains Ranch right after school. Her expression was joyful, but seconds later turned sour when she, with a sleepy face, looked into the mirror and burst out in an angry voice:

"Maxwell, what's wrong with you - why are you not coming?" she squinted her eyes and frowned, "Could he hate me so much he doesn't want to be with me?" She didn't have time for an answer before her mom yelled from downstairs,

"Breakfast!... Breakfast is served!"

It wasn't a good day at school. Rebekah was in another world, and so short-tempered she ignored Alexander's excitement about the trip. He had asked his mom to keep his backpack, his clothes, and all his excursion paraphernalia in the car so he could change into his new explorer uniform during the ride. They planned to rush to the Harkens' residence right after school. They were told to hurry as Rebekah's dad wanted to take off as soon as possible in the afternoon to reach his camping destination before dusk.

192

Maxwell did not even look at Rebekah, or maybe on a few occasions tried to send her a smile; a gesture she totally ignored. When Maxwell did not even show up for the last class she got really mad because she was sure he had gone right to the sports field with the bimbo cheerleader girls whom she hated.

"He could at least have wished us a nice trip," she sneered to Alexander.

When the old church bell rang, everyone quickly disappeared without any further talking.

"See you soon," Alexander whispered as he passed her in the staircase rushing out. But she was still so mad that she didn't even answer him; really, she was so angry she wanted to skip the entire trip.

When Alexander's mom reached the Harkens' house the family's big SUV was already packed, ready for departure, and Alexander had changed into his explorer uniform with his Mr. Z paraphernalia. They parked on the side of the driveway so as not to block the SUV, and greeted Mr. Harkens and Jonathan who were attaching a trailer to it. The twins weren't going; they were staying with friends for the break. Rebekah's mom came out and greeted Mrs. King with a big smile and a hug. Rebekah came downstairs soon after, dressed sharply in her black jeans, which she had stuck into her explorer boots, a blouse, her power belt, and a well-fitted red leather jacket, great for an excursion. She carried her Mr. Z knapsack in her left hand and her power wand in her right. She was now ballistic mad and barely said hello.

Then a big yellow Ford sedan pulled up right behind Mrs. King's car. Rebekah turned around and saw Maxwell and his mom. Boy was she surprised. Her sour face immediately turned into a sunshine smile of happiness.

"Maxwell!!!" she screamed, "you're coming?!!"

"Yeah," he smirked, "Yeah," he repeated, "I'm very excited to go on this wonderful excursion."

"What happened?" she gulped back.

"Well," he smiled, "my mom, your mom and Alexander's mom all got together, and here I am."

They all laughed as they climbed into the back of the SUV along with Rebekah's dog Prince.

*   *   *

They quickly moved out of Forrestville and followed the sun toward the west. Rebekah's family had always lived in this area and her dad knew all the shortcuts and unmarked roads up through the mountain pass.

Rebekah's great, great, great grandfather had emigrated from Scotland and was a very hard-working man. He was a clergyman, and bought land all over the west, since his dad had taught him to buy land to build security against bad times. As he also realized the need for education, he started the Forrestville Academy. Her great, great grandfather was very smart and an outstanding businessman who became a leader in coal mining, and later, in oil exploration. He discovered oil on the Harkens land, soon becoming very rich, and went into banking as well. His son helped him develop the oil and coal business and expanded the Harkens' Forrestville Academy by building more buildings and towers to attract more students, so as to educate more young people to become scientists and leaders.

Her great, great granddad purchased a ranch in the Uthea Mountains and later bought a magnificent German-Swiss castle and moved it, stone by stone, to the mountain ranch at the Uthea estate at the end of the 18th century. The Harkens Dynasty still owned the Uthea Canyon Ranch and Rebekah loved to go out there with her dad as often as she could. Rebekah's granddad lived in a mighty estate in Forrestville but did not love the ranch as much as his son. He was very focused on running the Academy and educating the youth.

The ranch had horses and cows and it was run as a ranch; part of it was wild and other parts contained numerous oil pumps which could be seen all over the Harkens' western prairie. They looked like big dinosaurs moving their heads up and down as the black gold was pumped out of the ground.

Besides being a smart businessman, Rebekah's dad was an explorer and an inventor. He collaborated with Mr. Z to develop special oil drills and many robotic instruments. Mr. Z and her dad also developed the unique convertible camping trailer they pulled behind the car, that could be folded to being only a few feet tall but could expand to become a full-sized camping vehicle.

The Harkens SUV pulled the large trailer through the scenic terrain with its green swooping acres and huge green trees. Bison, buffalo, cows, deer, and horses added living colors to the picturesque countryside.

* * *

When they took off on the journey the sun was high on the horizon toward the southwest and Mr. Harkens drove through many magnificent backroads. It was a trip full of surprises, and the kids very happily inhaled the glorious views. They laughed, talked, and were excited until late in the afternoon, when, fatigued, they fell asleep.

They drove until after dusk, when it suddenly became pitch black, except for the stars lighting up the sky. They were in the mountains and after some time Mr. Harkens pulled the SUV into a campsite he had stayed at many times before. The bumpy mountain road violently tossed the SUV from side to side, waking up the startled kids, who immediately became super happy.

They bounded out of the SUV. Alexander noted the stars which looked large against the silhouette of the mountains. This was the first time he ever had been away from his house and out into nature. He inhaled deeply, closed his eyes, and thanked God for being so good to him.

The convertible trailer was, with the push of a few buttons, turned into a full-sized mobile home with a kitchen, bathroom, and sitting room. They unfolded a tent from the back and soon had a great camping complex at their disposal. They raised a smaller tent for Alexander and Maxwell next to the Harkens' own. Jonathan found a fire-pit and started a fire sending relaxing waves of heat toward the tents, and flames that seemed to reach up to the small cumulous clouds drifting by, which occasionally obstructed the glittering stars. Rebekah's mom started to prepare a meal and Jonathan, with Prince, his faithful labrador, at his tail, invited Alexander to join him to inspect the premises. Alexander looked at Rebekah as if to ask if she wanted to join them. She quickly waved a 'no thank you'. She was very happy sitting alone with her 'man' Maxwell, next to the blazing fire!

Jonathan pointed out a few other tents and mobile homes along the forest-covered mountain ridge. One couple had erected their tent behind a group of trees and an older couple, sitting outside their tent not far from Rebekah's dad's tent complex, waved to them.

Then Jonathan noticed a few suspicious looking dudes sneaking around the tents and an old run-down Ford parked on the other side of the dirt road.

Jonathan gave Alexander a high sign to kneel down as they carefully observed the 'dudes'.

"They're up to something," whispered Jonathan. "Probably druggies and thieves," he continued in a low voice as they saw two of the dudes disappear into the trees. Prince surged toward them. He was a smart and curious sleuth…

Suddenly they heard rattling in the bushes. Prince rushed out from behind the trees speeding like a bullet right toward one of the more suspicious dudes. The dudes sprinted toward their old Ford, with Prince racing toward them but the most suspicious looking dude did not make it in time. Prince attacked and wrestled him to the ground. Prince was just about to sink his teeth into the neck of the dude, when Jonathan, moving fast, arrived. "Stop Prince!!! Prince let go!!! "he screamed. Prince stopped. Jonathan yelled at the dudes. "Get out of here!"

Just then the old Ford drove on to the forest dirt road with one door open, a pair of hands pulled the dude into it, then it sped off.

Prince was a great watchdog and they all went to sleep knowing they were protected by a great guard…

*   *   *

But later, in the middle of the starry night, loud and scary barks echoed from an angry Prince, that made Jonathan and Mr. Harkens rush out of their tent. Alexander heard the commotion and quickly grabbed his power wand and rushed outside too. He sped off on Jonathan's heels following Prince. They stumbled into a thick forest grove just in time to see Prince attacking one of the dudes they had chased away that evening.

One of the dudes screamed, running as fast as he could and dropping something behind him. Another dude ran the other way scared to death. He dropped a red bag. Prince attacked one dude and wrestled him to the ground just as Jonathan and Alexander arrived.

"I'm sorry! I'm sorry!" the dude cried, covering his face with his hands while lying on the ground in a fetal position to protect his throat against Prince's fearsome bite. The dude cried like a baby, "I promise never again - never, uhh, never again!" he continued.

Alexander used the power light on his wand and found the red bag. Soon after, he located the other bag. Both contained money and personal ID's.

"They're thieves! There's money and other stuff in the sacks," Alexander informed Jonathan.

"Prince let go!" yelled Jonathan, and the furious dog let go. Jonathan was right on top of the dude and he kicked him in his behind several times. "Get out of here!!" he screamed, "or I will call the cops! Never come back!" Prince snarled angrily baring his teeth. Alexander took a picture of the dude pinned down by the mighty Prince. The beaten-up dude crawled to his feet and took off running for his life toward his car. The old Ford scurried away, puffing and blowing smoke all the way down the narrow dirt road.

Rebekah's dad searched the area and discovered the open trunk of the car belonging to the old couple they had met that evening. The old veteran was climbing out of his tent, awakened by all the commotion and the barking dog. Sure enough, the couple's car had been broken into, and the couple was very grateful to Alexander when he returned their stolen bags. A few hours later, when the sun sent its bright morning rays over the mountaintops and into their camp, William Harkens IV rose and came out of his tent to inspect the surroundings. They all had breakfast, and at the top of the morning, took off on the final leg of their trip to The Big Canyon Ranch.

*   *   *

The ride was amazing. They moved along scenic back roads and passed awesome mountains and valleys. Rebekah pointed out large herds of buffalo guarded by cowboys, and amazing scenic views that mesmerized the boys. The sun rose higher in the sky and sent ever-changing shadows into the valleys and prairies, making the landscape somehow mystical.

They finally turned off the narrow back road and into a more open road lined with large trees. Soon they noticed an old sign - 'The Canyon Ranch' – pointing to

the right. The family SUV with its RV- trailer, soon
reached a well-paved road, and they eventually drove up
to a large antique iron gate.

It was impressively crafted with two separate large
swinging doors constructed from hand-made iron rods.
Each square was covered with green iron-crafted leaves.
The gates' hinges were attached to two large limestone
columns that were completely overgrown with green
ivy. Each stone column was decorated on top with a
large sculptured eagle lantern. On top, a large curved
iron frame stretched like a rainbow between the two
limestone columns.

A large ivy leaf decorated the iron-cast frame and a
black iron sign declared... **'BIG CANYON RANCH'**.

"Astonishing," blurted Alexander.

Mr. Harkens drove up close to the gate and pushed an
almost-hidden button.

"Can I help you?" a voice responded.

"Mr. Harkens," he answered with a deep voice.

Rebekah and her mom vigorously waved their hands
close to the windshield to get the staff's attention. They
knew they were watching on a hidden camera. Soon
after they heard happy excitement through the intercom
system.

"Welcome back Mr. and Mrs. Harkens," an excited
voice responded. The staff adored the family.

The majestic gate swung open and they drove up an
asphalt road lined with beautiful trees. It was a far cry
from the dirt roads they had driven earlier.

* * *

The Harkens Canyon estate road twisted and turned through a magnificent landscape. The road was very peaceful; birds singing, the background sound of 'music' from the big trees swaying in  the wind with their leaves fluttering. All sounding as if they were singing, 'welcome back'.

Alexander noticed several houses set way back from the road, so they did not clutter the view. The houses were of various bright colors mixing beautifully into the landscape. Alexander saw a few cars parked behind them and as he got closer, heard kids playing.

"What a wonderful way to grow up," he thought to himself. So different from his large haunted wooden house, and the fact that he never had siblings to play with.

"Those are the staff houses," Rebekah broke the silence. She noticed Alexander's and Maxwell's curiosity.

"It must be so nice to live here," Alexander remarked.

"Yes," Rebekah responded, "it is lovely."

The road twisted again, then made a few sharp turns through a mountain pass; then a very sharp left turn followed right after by another steep right, as they cut through a narrow mountain pass and entered an open observation platform on the other side the mountain. It was a natural observation plateau; a panorama of the entire glorious valley lay in front of them.

It was a picture so magical so mystical, that Alexander's heart almost stopped.

"Wow!" he exclaimed, as he rose in his seat and leaned forward to get a clearer picture of the awesome cycloramic view in front of his eyes.

"Yes awesome, real awesome," Maxwell echoed.

"Yes, it's something, isn't it?" Mrs. Harkens said with a smile, "We love this place".

"I have never seen such magnificence before," Alexander nodded, as he inhaled the theatrical glittering landscape spread out in front of them. Then, in the midst of this astonishing scene, there arose a castle with tall towers and impressive spires, all seemingly reaching the sky.

Maxwell and Alexander, speechless for minutes, studied the architecture of this historical castle that appeared to penetrate the clouds. It was built on a cliff rising behind the expansive lush valley right beneath them.

The road then twisted and turned as they drove down the steep mountain pass until they arrived at the large green valley. It was an amazing savannah. Rivers ran through it and large herds of buffalo, wild horses, bison, deer, and many other animals they could not even recognize, roamed freely. It was an enormous natural zoo.

They crossed an old river bridge and soon the landscape began to elevate into more rugged terrain as they got closer to the awesome, enormous castle. The rocks broke through the green grass and now they saw no more tall trees. The land had been cleared so enemies couldn't hide from the fortress' towers.

The landscape elevated into a mountain and right in front of them the castle rose like a huge pinnacle of pride. The castle was bordered by four tall towers; one in each corner of the large citadel, with golden steeples reaching to the sky in a show of mystical power. The spires, the top of the steeples, were so tall they seemed to disappear into the cumulus clouds as they reached high into the air.

A few slimmer but taller towers were incorporated into the castle's architecture, each with glorious steeples and golden spires glittering in the sun. The castle's walls were covered with ivy that beautified it even more. It was a spectacular castle, of a might, the boys had never before experienced. They were mesmerized and awed by the splendor of the magnificent constellation unfolding before their eyes.

The road soon brought them so close to the castle that Alexander noticed a moat and a hanging wooden drawbridge. Their access would be prohibited unless the drawbridge was let down. One would need an army to get into this place, Alexander thought to himself.

As they got closer the boys noticed many more unbelievable details about the Uthea castle.

Rebekah saw their curiosity and began to explain.

"This castle is our family pride. My dad calls it our ranch because he keeps lots of animals. He has a horse breeding unit and racehorses, and he runs part of the estate as a dairy farm, and part of it as a horse farm. There are also chickens, ducks, and pigs. The most rugged part of the estate is used for oil extraction. Daddy owns some of the most successful oil producing wells in this district. You will see the oil pumps and fracking machines," she continued as she gestured.

"My great-great-great granddad was an educated man who came to America from Europe. He knew everything about the newest farming and animal breeding techniques; he was also a clergyman, well educated in chemistry and veterinary science. He began to breed horses and sold them to Native Americans for land. That was how this ranch grew so big. The old William Harkens was very clever and, like President George Washington before him, used European farming methods to make his farms successful. He made lots of money selling corn, meat and other produce, but like President Washington he also made money from whiskey and other strong spirits that he made from grains," smiled Rebekah, as she pointed to a herd of wild horses galloping over the prairie.

"When he couldn't find enough educated staff to work at his ranches and industries, he decided the country needed to educate its children in a more sophisticated manner, handed over leadership of his holdings to his son, and started Forrestville Academy. He was the first teacher at the school." The boys smiled in amazement as they kept looking at the prodigious mammoth castle rising in front of them glittering in the powerful afternoon sun. Alexander sent a silent 'thank you' to his 'friend' - the painting of William Marshall Harkens!

"The old William and his sons," continued Rebekah, became very rich and bought more and more land. Later, they even found major oil deposits stretching under this wild land out here in Uthea. This made the family very wealthy and they started a very large banking empire as well," she paused a moment, "My great, great grandfather," continued Rebekah, "William Junior, traveled to Europe, fell in love with European castles, and bought this magnificent castle in the Bavarian Alps, a magnified replica of a famous gothic Scottish Castle. He loved it so much he moved it here like the famous publisher Randolph H. Hearst did in California. My great, great granddad moved his Bavarian castle stone by stone, all the way out here to the Uthea Mountains, where he had the colossal structure rebuilt."

Rebekah laughed like a circus announcer and pointed toward the glorious castle.

"Voila – William Harkens Junior's dream!"

They nodded and smiled in unison. "Yes, it was an unbelievable task. Every stone was marked and shipped. My great grandfather never took no for an answer," Mr. Harkens proudly remarked.

"The castle looks like it belongs out here," Alexander said.

"You are right, Alexander," Mrs. Harkens broke in, "now it belongs out here," she smiled.

"Money was never a problem for the old man. He built the most awesome buildings anyone has ever seen," smiled Jonathan.

*   *   *

ENTERING THE CASTLE

They continued through the picturesque landscape, and soon got close to the hanging drawbridge.

Alexander realized that the side of the moat closest to the castle rose up into a high grass-covered wall originally constructed to protect the castle by helping soldiers defend it against intruders.

The drawbridge had been pulled up and Alexander saw Mr. Harkens stick his arm out the window and wave. Jonathan did the same. Soon after, the wooden drawbridge began to lower so they could pass over the moat.

The old hanging drawbridge was made of wooden beams. It made a singing sound as they drove over it. The road led up to a large door in the middle of the eastern wing of the gigantic building. Maxwell smiled in awe.

The large door swung open, courtesy of a few of the castle's male staffers manually opening it as Mr. Harkens drove into the Uthea castle.

The driveway was paved with cobblestones brought over from Europe with the castle, stone by stone. The SUV moved slowly through the gate into the circular cobblestone drive inside the castle courtyard. A big impressive oak tree was located in the center protected by a circular iron fence. Four towers, one in each corner, raised their steeples into the sky. Three to four storied large brick buildings connected the towers while other tall towers were built into the castle adding to its might and mystique. The walls and towers were overgrown with ivy that climbed and covered all the walls. Alexander was impressed to be sure.

*   *   *

THE AWESOME CASTLE

Alexander was so flabbergasted he rolled down the window and stuck his head out to get a better view and to absorb it; to breathe in the air.

Rebekah was pleased with Maxwell's and Alexander's fascination with 'her ranch'. She had finally impressed Maxwell. She inhaled with pride.

"It is awesome, isn't it?" asked Rebekah.

"It is awesome," replied Alexander, "Now I see why my mom wanted me to go with you," Maxwell added shaking his head in disbelief.

"Can you imagine what a job it must have been to move this all the way from Europe, brick by brick and beam by beam?" Rebekah said, "I will show you guys some pictures of the amazing undertaking," she continued.

"I hope you will have a nice time," Rebekah's mother told the boys.

"I love it already," replied Alexander.

"Me too," seconded Maxwell.

"The west wing is over there," Rebekah pointed, "that's where we live. The horses are kept in the south wing. The dogs are also in the south wing, over there," Rebekah pointed out. "I can hear the dogs," smiled Alexander, as the dogs sent welcoming barks through the air. "The cows and other animals are kept in the north wing," Rebekah explained, "Staff quarters and the offices are on the higher floors," she pointed upwards.

*   *   *

They slowly drove around the big oak tree on the cobblestones. The SUV and the trailer danced over the stone-paved circular drive. Alexander noted the castle's staff members at the doors at the west wing, all in uniform. They waved as the SUV got closer to the residential wing. Two Rhodesian Ridgeback hunting dogs raced toward them; Mr. Harkens' private hunting dogs whom he had rescued from a shelter in Chicago. "This is McCarthy and McKnight," said Rebekah's dad with a smile as the dogs reached the SUV. It was a remarkable welcome!

*   *   *

ALEXANDER'S ROYAL SUITE

A butler carried Alexander's luggage – his knapsack – to his sleeping quarters on the second floor. Another butler followed and brought Maxwell's belongings upstairs to his quarters down the hall from Alexander's room.

"This is the master bedroom suite," Alexander's butler explained as they passed the first-floor landing, "it leads to the Harkens' private residence." It was one level above the ground floor. The butler walked up to the next landing and led Alexander into his room. He was mesmerized at what he saw. He had never seen a bedroom like this! "Awesome," he whispered to himself as he looked around. The room was in royal blue and gold colors, with a thick carpet and with blue and red curtains.

The bed was a large king-size bed, with four bed posts and golden and red draperies stretched between the tops of the bed posts, and a decorated valance reaching down the sides. He jumped on to the bed. It was so big he felt like a midget on a football field. He then went into the bathroom. It was majestic too, with thick royal blue and gold carpet and a very large antique-looking bathtub with golden faucets shaped like swans.

All the faucets were antique with golden swans. It was impressive and elegant.

Alexander took a quick shower and changed his clothes. He donned his favorite explorer jeans and his power sneakers. His mother had packed his favorite blue shirt with his name embroidered on the right sleeve pocket. He placed the shirt outside his pants and donned his power belt outside the shirt. He looked in the big mirror and smiled; he was getting more self-confidence.

Alexander then looked out of the windows. There was a small balcony outside and he walked out on it. An awesome panoramic view greeted him. The grass lawn stretched and curved way down toward a lake and mountains in the distance. The lawns were well manicured, with beautiful trees and bushes on both sides stretching downward towards the lake. A large fountain was splashing water on to a massive sculpture of what appeared to be wild horses. There was a large sitting area outside the castle, where he noticed a large stone table and a built-in grill stove to the right.

A large swimming pool was twisting its borders among the rocks and bushes where a small stream ran into the pool. Beautiful tiles and grass ran along the circumference. A pool house stretched around the left part of the pool where he saw tables and sofas. It was elegant; beauty mixed with nature in a harmonious way. Alexander looked back at his room. He loved it. It was lavish. It made him feel very special.

*   *   *

A few minutes later, a butler knocked at the door. "Lunch is served on the verandah in five minutes, Sir," the butler announced. Alexander couldn't believe his ears; he was called 'Sir'. He was so stunned he couldn't respond. "Do you read me, Sir?" the butler repeated louder, "Do you hear me now?" The butler almost yelled. Alexander calmed down, "Yeah!" Alexander responded in a low voice as he walked closer to the door. The butler repeated, "Lunch is served, Sir."

"OK!' Alexander almost whispered. He then cleared his throat, "Yes, thank you!" he repeated with a louder voice that seemed to get lost in the large room. He then repeated his response with a clear loud, confident voice. "Yes, Sir, I will be there, thank you Sir!"

*   *   *

Alexander looked around with wide eyes. He smiled - bent forward, flexed his right arm and fisted his hand. "Yeah!" he screamed as he jumped in the air with joy. He jumped up again and again, fisted his hands, flexed his arms and moved his legs as if he was biking. "Yeah," he declared. The butler called him 'Sir'. This was the first time in his life he was called 'Sir'. People were finally accepting him as a real person. He had arrived!

Still exhilarated, Alexander looked around. There was a painting of a general on one wall; one of Rebekah's forefathers probably. A general's ornate uniform and hat hung next to the portrait. Alexander could not help himself. He placed two chairs on top of each other, climbed up, fetched the hat and donned the general's cap almost tumbling to the floor. He then climbed up on the tall antique Burgermeister chair leaning against the opposite wall. Although he looked ridiculous with the big hat almost covering his eyes, he proudly crossed his arms and sat down like a royal prince. With his arms crossed over his chest, he looked out and felt very proud and important. Although he looked like a Hobbit on the gigantic chair, Alexander felt as proud as a king.

*   *   *

FAMILY LUNCH ON THE VERANDAH

Maxwell was already at the table next to Rebekah when Alexander finally arrived.

"Welcome to Big Canyon Ranch," Rebekah's mother and father wished Alexander, when he entered.

"Thank you so much for inviting me," Alexander responded, as a butler approached.

"What can I serve you?" the butler asked. "Alexander was hungry, nervous and insecure, but Rebekah saved him from making a stupid mistake…

"We would both like a glass of mango juice with

ice," she ordered.

Alexander was relieved.

* * *

It was an impressive lunch with all the food one could desire, served out on the stunning verandah on a table set with silver platters, antique British China and real silverware. Three butlers, all dressed in white tuxedo jacket uniforms, served the six of them. Alexander had never dined at a first-class restaurant much less this. He was blown away.

* * *

After lunch, Mrs. Harkens invited the kid's poolside for after-lunch tea. They walked over the lawn down to the swimming pool and sat down under the verandah part of the pool house on plush chairs and sofas with large antique pillows. The pool water was so sky-blue the butlers' reflections in it were mirror clear when they passed close by.

It was such a thrilling experience. Alexander had never seen such a panorama.

"Dad!" said Rebekah, "Can me and the boys go and look at the horses?" "Yes, of course," responded Mr. Harkens.

"Jonathan, please take them there."

"Dad, should I give Alexander a horse?" asked Jonathan.

"Yes, give him a nice pony," his father smiled.

They walked through the west wing into the courtyard next to the big oak tree toward the horse wing. Alexander smiled.

"They are so nice," he thought to himself, "they are giving me a horse." He saw himself riding his horse on the back roads in Forrestville with Pluto at his heels; Pluto and his horse racing each other. A dream comes true.

Rebekah, Maxwell and Jonathan went into the stable. Alexander was still in dreamland 'riding his new horse,' when the stable door again opened and Rebekah yelled to him, "Where are you Alexander? Hurry up!"

The Yellow Flag

THE HORSE STABLE

The stable was packed with all kinds of horses. They were small and big, racing and hunting horses. Alexander was stunned. This was his first visit to a ranch and now he was seeing things he never imagined. Friendly stable hands welcomed them, and Jonathan led them to the area in the stable where the stalls contained only ponies. The stable master greeted them, and Jonathan explained to him what they were looking for.

Rebekah was dressed in her explorer outfit with her Mr. Z power-belt on the outside of her lavender shirt over her black jeans which were tucked inside her high sporty calypso colored sneakers. The sneakers were colorful; violet, blue, and orange, lined with lime-green, black, and yellow stripes.

She had attached her power wand as well as her white shade cap, to the belt. Her mother had packed a picnic box in case they got hungry during their ride, and Rebekah had put the food inside her green backpack and put on her burgundy leather belt before strapping on the backpack. Maxwell wore his jeans tucked inside his dark red and yellow soccer sneakers. He wore a sporty white T-shirt engraved with the word 'winner' on the front, and a dark blue sports-jacket with white stripes at the bottom and on the arms. The power-belt supported his back. A Forrestville sports emblem was embossed on his left jacket pocket and he had donned his school team's baseball cap. When he saw that the others had brought their power wands and backpacks, he ran back to his room to fetch his.

Alexander had carefully dressed himself in the black jeans his mom had bought and tucked them inside the magic power sneakers Mr. Z had made for him. The sneakers were decorated with multiple bright colors and were decorated with  reflective color stripes. He wore a black shirt and his beloved power-belt was strapped around his waist with his miracle wand attached to his belt on the left side, and his explorer knife on the right. His mom had also bought him a fiery red sports-jacket with black stripes and a hood, which had a long zipper so he could close it right up to his neck to withstand rough weather. The word 'Explorer' was engraved in dark blue letters on the back.

He had Mr. Z's special backpack that contained all the explorer paraphernalia one could ever imagine and had attached the shade hat to it that Mr. Z had given him.

"We'll go get horses for the boys," Jonathan suggested. "Maxwell and Rebekah can ride, so they'll get horses, but since Alexander hasn't been on a horse, he should ride a pony."

Oh, how silly of me, thought Alexander, I thought they were giving me a horse, but they're just lending me a pony. But how nice of them to consider that I'm new at this.

Rebekah chose a smaller white horse for herself. It was already saddled up, so she jumped on with a little help from a stable hand, rode slowly out the back door then galloped down the training field. The stable-master found a similar black-and-brown horse for Maxwell, who mounted with elegance and ease and galloped away after Rebekah.

Alexander went outside. He watched his friends with a little envy. She's good at everything as is Maxwell. He's great at all sorts of sports. He had a lot to learn, but that was fine; he had lots of time.

Jonathan was back from his first run. He was an excellent equestrian. He jumped off the horse and asked one of the stable hands to hold it.

*   *   *

Jonathan helped Alexander choose his pony and gave him basic riding instructions. They had gone to the stable and the stable master had picked out a black-and-white striped pony for him. "It's a beautiful pony. Let's call her 'Black and White'," beamed Alexander, and both Jonathan and the stable-master smiled. "I'll get you a good saddle, so you don't have to worry about your style," explained Jonathan. They walked the pony to grooming area where Jonathan helped Alexander up and strolled with him on the pony for a few rounds, until he felt secure. Then, walking the pony beside Jonathan down to the field, they spotted Rebekah on her way back.

"You're doing great Alexander," she called out to him. She really appreciated Alexander because she knew that if he hadn't come along, neither would have Maxwell.

*   *   *

Jonathan galloped down the hill through the scenic landscape with horses behind fences on both sides of the path and caught up with Maxwell. Rebekah caught up with the two of them shortly after, but Alexander was riding alone and was slow and insecure. He was afraid he'd fall off Black and White, so he couldn't look up and hoped the pony knew where she was going. Rebekah saw his fear, turned around, and galloped back to join him, and they rode down the mountain slopes together. The towers looked very impressive against the blue sky up on the hill. and the horses behind the fences followed them and galloped back and forth as if paving the way and guarding their walk as they slowly descended toward the lake.

"Look at those unique birds!" said Rebekah, pointing at a flock of very small birds. But Alexander was too scared to look up and stared at the back of his pony's head, praying that she wouldn't lurch forward. They moved slowly and steadily as they passed the horses that galloped back and forth behind the fence, then the field opened up and they met a small group of wild horses. Rebekah tried to take his mind off his own pony by telling Alexander about the history of the wild horses, but he wasn't listening; too scared that he was going to slide off the saddle, as he was sliding from one side to the other. He was new at this and hoped he'd relax soon and stop stiffening up. Rebekah explained that the pony could feel his fear, so he definitely needed to relax.

"If this is the wrong horse for you, tomorrow we'll try another one," she tried to calm him. Alexander wasn't ready to give up. He was going to relax and build up his courage; isn't that what growing up was all about? When they got to the lake they met up with Jonathan, Maxwell, and some of the staff. He was helped off the pony and was very relieved, but he was determined to become a real equestrian.

*		*		*

THE PHOSPHORESCENT LIT CAVE

The staff helped Jonathan push the boat into the lake. They had tied the kids' horses to a tree near the lake and had given them life jackets and helped them get into the boat. Jonathan started the motor and they took off on their next adventure through the narrow parts of the lake. This was where they would find birds in their natural habitats. Jonathan soon killed the motor and they drifted slowly down the lake which was filled with ducks, swans, and many more species of birds that the kids have never seen before. The water mirrored the bright sun and occasionally Jonathan started up the motor and changed direction as he moved the boat into the bigger lake ahead. An hour later he altered their route again and moved slowly toward the mountains that rose out of the water.

It was a terrific journey and Jonathan was an excellent guide. He pointed out the uniqueness and intricacies of the mountains and explained that they were actually headed toward the Rocky Mountains.

Jonathan had brought some binoculars and he handed them to Alexander and Maxwell, directing their attention toward a big opening at the bottom of the mountain ahead that was reaching to the level of the water's surface.

"What is that?" asked Alexander and Maxwell.

"It's the opening to a mysterious cave I wanted you to see. We should be there soon," said Jonathan smiling in anticipation.

*   *   *

He kept pointing out the canyons in front of them. The view took Alexander's breath away. It was much more impressive than in the photos he saw on the Internet. Maxwell was amazed too. Rebekah took his hand and smiled at him. The beauty and the serenity of the trip was astounding.

"It's beautiful, isn't it?" she spoke quietly. Maxwell nodded.

As they approached the mountain ridge, Alexander noticed how clear the cliff's reflection was in the lake. He looked up to see the mountains standing upright and reaching into the few clouds that hovered over the lake and seemed to be circling over the mountain tops. It was all so amazing.

He recalled how Professor Finley had described the shifts in the earth's layers that resulted in more mountains, canyons, and lakes being formed. It all made sense to him. He saw the cliffs differently now.

*   *   *

The boat hit some rocks that had collapsed around the entrance to the cave and Jonathan did some zigzagging to get into the entrance. Jonathan described how caves were created by the shifts and folding of the earth's layers. "So many caverns are blocked by collapsed rocks and people believe that we could be finding many secret caves and some wildlife that we haven't seen before. He moved the boat deeper towards the cavern.

*   *   *

The cavern was alive; illuminated with a variety of colorful fish and some creepy water monsters. "It's weird, isn't it?" Rebekah called out. Everyone made a guttural sound as Jonathan killed the motor, and they drifted into this magical area. There were some wild sounds; fish were jumping high out of the water and racing as if they were being chased. The cave was a soft greenish shade and it all looked scary to the kids. But they moved on, sometimes hearing animal sounds emanating from the shore. Rebekah heard some noise that scared her, and she grabbed Jonathan's arm. A frightening scream ripped through the air.

Alexander couldn't keep his eyes off the water, especially since they had all noticed some of the cave monsters behind the boat… just a bit too close for their liking. Alexander whispered, "Are we safe? We're being followed," and pointed into the green water about five feet away.

"I know," replied Jonathan, "I have seen them. This place is filled with some mysterious monsters." "What's causing the greenish-blue light in here?" Alexander asked no one in particular.

"The cave walls are packed with a phosphoric waxy chemical which gives off phosphorescence; greenish light, almost like the hands of a clock in the dark," explained Jonathan, as he turned the boat around and sailed out of the cavern.

*   *   *

They were anxious to get back on the horses and ride back up to the castle. As they were mounting their horses Alexander thanked Jonathan for taking them on such a fascinating journey. It was a very special experience, but so far everything about this trip was more than he ever expected.

"There are so many of these caves and caverns on our property," said Rebekah, as she was getting on her horse, "We'll be going on a hunt tomorrow and you'll see more of them," she said excitedly and proudly.

"Are there many animals in these caves?" asked Alexander, somewhat surprised.

"Yes, some of these big caves look like giant zoos, with all kinds of animals and reptiles, and even monsters," responded Jonathan as he galloped off.

"It's still early. Let me take you on a little trip around the valley near the mountain edge. You'll like the landscape and the real beauty of nature," Rebekah said enthusiastically.

"Great," the boys replied in unison. Rebekah enjoyed her outing with the boys, and just chatting with Maxwell, who was becoming very comfortable hanging out with her. She was glad that Alexander was still uncomfortable on his pony and would be falling behind.

Alexander was getting more comfortable and occasionally made the pony gallop for a minute or two. Riding was more fun so he didn't bother to rush. He was happy skipping along with White and Black. The others were accomplished riders and one day he would be one too.

*　　*　　*

The 'Three Musketeers' as they liked to call themselves, continued along a winding road toward the canyon that Rebekah wanted to show off.

They looked like a group of cowboys as they rode comfortably together and enjoyed the valley and the landscape that looked to them as if they were in the middle of a painting. It was far more impressive than anything he had seen in his books... even the ones in his dad's library.

They were a team now. Rebekah took care and looked back to make sure that Alexander was all right. She really liked Alexander and was happy that this was a trip he would never forget. She also enjoyed competing with Maxwell on this ride. They circled around each other then raced to an object and did it again. They could see Alexander falling back so they rode back a little and started the competition again, not moving too far ahead. Alexander was starting to speed up but then his pony jumped and raised her front hoof.

She had been scared by a rabbit that crossed her path.

But Alexander wasn't prepared for this and the weight of his knapsack propelled him forward and he slid off the pony, flipped, and landed on top of his backpack in the mud beside a rock. He was very fortunate to have landed in the mud. If he had hit the rock, he would have been hurt.

"Sugar!" Alexander had called out, but no one heard him. His body wasn't hurt but his pride was. He tried to get up but kept slipping into the mud and slowly began to sink. He slipped off his knapsack, found the lasso rope in his sack and threw it toward the rock. His first attempt failed but he succeeded on his next attempt and he slowly pulled himself out of the mud. This is when Maxwell noticed that Alexander's pony was standing still... but no Alexander. He was worried and raced back with Rebekah following behind. They jumped down and helped him get out of the mud.

"You OK?" asked a breathless Rebekah.

"Yeah, I am," he nodded, a little touchy.

Rebekah was so relieved she started to laugh and tried to help Alexander relax. It had been a scare. "You look so funny with your face covered in mud. Let's go down to the stream and get you washed up," she suggested. They mounted their horses and rode off to the mountain stream which happened to be surrounded by a bed of rocks that formed chairs. They climbed off their horses, tied them up, and went over to the stream to wash. Maxwell noticed that the stream started at a waterfall at the foot of the rocks, and it looked clean and very inviting.

"You thirsty Alexander?" he called back to him as he ran forward toward the waterfall.

"I sure am," Alexander replied, and they climbed over the rocks to the fresh mountain 'faucet'. They created cups out of their palms and drank the cold, natural water. They playfully sprayed each other and laughed.

The musketeers sat down and took out the food boxes Rebekah's mom had prepared for them. They ate the delicious salami and cheese sandwiches and enjoyed the fresh fruit. They rested and chatted for a while then got back on their horses and rode further into the wilderness. Rebekah knew the area well, having crisscrossed and explored it many times, and was confident to take them further into the canyon. She wanted them to experience the most picturesque views they would ever see.

* * *

THE SCARY FOX CAVE

It was a balmy and clear afternoon as the musketeers continued to ride downhill and into another canyon. The sun was peeking over the mountains from the southwest and they continued to ride through a canyon crevice lined by tall cliffs on both sides. They crossed the valley and rode toward the fox cave that Rebekah wanted to show them.

They entered the cave and moved carefully towards the corner. The collapsed rocks formed a wall between several connecting caves. The entrance was very narrow, so they tied their horses to the rocks and took off their backpacks to rest and to have a cold drink.

"Do you know what's inside, Rebekah?" mumbled Maxwell.

"I always thought that this cave was the home to foxes," said Rebekah. She tested her cell phone to make sure she had connection by dialing Christiana. When Christiana picked up, Rebekah said, "It's me!" She had to yell to be heard at the other end. It was impossible for the boys to follow a conversation between the two chatty girls.

Alexander and Maxwell took off their backpacks, grabbed their power wands and with the help of the light from the wands, they climbed inside the narrow hole. Alexander was first to enter. He had to crawl on his stomach and keep the light shining ahead of them, and eventually they saw the big cave open before them.

"Come on," Alexander called out, so Maxwell knew his location, and Maxwell followed. The cave was much wider now and Alexander could stand up for a while but soon he had to get back on his stomach as the tunnel narrowed again. Maxwell had barely entered the wider area and was about to drop back down on his stomach when he heard a loud yelp followed by one scream and then another. Then Maxwell was hit from behind, and he fell to the ground. He had time to reach for his wand

and open it as a knife. The attacker was a fury–breathing monster which then kicked the wand-knife out of his hand.

The attack happened so fast and when he tried to stand up, he was struck again and again by the yelping monster. Then another monster came out from a hole in the wall and rushed at him. Maxwell was now really scared and his scream almost shattered Alexander's ear drums; he crouched on the ground and trembled when, yet another furry creature's body brushed over him. He covered his eyes to protect himself and pulled his legs up to his chest.

Alexander was scared because he didn't see the holes and hiding places that the monsters came out of. He pulled himself together, circled around, and pointed his power wand toward the fleeing animals. He caught a glimpse of the last monster and it appeared to be a weird looking fox. It didn't look so threatening; it looked like it was trying to hide from danger.

Alexander focused and beamed the light from the wand on the monsters who no longer looked dangerous. Then he swirled the wand around and looked for Maxwell who was still crouched in the corner looking as if he'd seen a ghost; his face bewildered. Alexander smiled and helped him up comforting him, saying that they were just foxes trying to save their own hides. They were as scared of the boys as the boys of them. Then he saw movement between the rocks inches away.

"Careful," he whispered, to Maxwell, "big snake…"

He focused the wand on the head of a large serpent. The creature was obviously disturbed by the foxes and Maxwell's screams. The boys knew that serpents could be dangerous and deadly, so Alexander kept his light focused directly on the serpent's head. The reptile was spellbound; hypnotized by the forceful beam from Mr. Z's power wand. Alexander knew that any noise could make the serpent attack one of them and he hoped that Maxwell wouldn't kick it either, because its bite could be fatal. Alexander pressed the emergency button on the wand which emitted a fearful, penetrating sound. Maxwell put his fingers in his ears. There were two buttons on the power wand, one louder and more penetrating than the other. Not knowing which was which, Alexander pushed the more powerful button. The penetrating sound was now mixed with a continuous high pitch, that was not perceptible to the human ear, but was very intense to animals. The high-pitched sound instilled fear into the creepy reptile and Maxwell turned his head just in time to see the venomous snake make a U-turn and disappear into the rocks. Maxwell recovered long enough to jump up, and rushed to the exit so fast he tumbled out like a dust ball, but in the rush he left his power wand and knife behind.

Rebekah had heard the wild screams and was moving quickly over toward the exit hole when she heard the emergency alarm and saw the last of the fleeing foxes rushing to safety around the side of the rocks. As she was peeking into the cave, she saw Maxwell crawling out of the hole and running like a dust ball. He dashed out and rolled on the ground. Rebekah looked on in amazement.

He got up, saw her looking at him, and was embarrassed. Her look changed from amazement to amusement. A big smile appeared on her face and they both laughed. She went over, helped him to his feet, dusted the dirt off his clothes, and continued to enjoy the moment.

"Don't laugh," Maxwell sounded a little annoyed, "I could have been killed."

"How so," she asked, not knowing what had happened in there.

"A huge dangerous serpent was about to attack me!" he exploded.

Rebekah felt admonished.

Alexander was feeling more and more like a warrior. What happened in that cave made him more self-confident, and he believed he reacted fast and strong. He had scanned the cave and found Maxwell's power wand and the other explorer equipment and walked out with an air of being sure of himself. He was calm, wiped off the dust on his pants, dusted Maxwell's power wand and equipment, and handed them to him.

"That was a close call, eh," Rebekah said.

"No, not especially," replied Alexander, who wasn't going to make a big deal of Maxwell's reaction. "We had Mr. Z's wand and alarm button and they can get us out of any situation," added Maxwell.

"Yeah, he's an amazing scientist and he's given us some powerful tools," Alexander explained. They all nodded and agreed that it was Mr. Z who had saved their lives.

They grabbed their knapsacks, went over to a group of rocks, sat down, took out their water bottles, and took a long drink, thinking about the dangers they had just avoided.

*   *   *

THE MYSTERIOUS MEN

The horses were excited to see their riders. The three musketeers had their attire, backpacks, wands, lights, knives... the whole paraphernalia, on their bodies. They grabbed the reins of the horses and mounted up. Alexander grabbed his cell phone and called his mother. He spoke with her excitedly, describing everything he'd done in the short time he'd been there. The musketeers strolled on their horses down a steep and narrow cliff, following closely behind each other. The sun was gone, and darkness was descending on them before they reached the narrowest part of the crevice. The view, even in the dark, was stunning. They rode up to the top and looked down at the world in all its splendor. The canyon opened up and they could see several hills and mountaintops in the distance, completely raw and naked. There was little foliage. They could also see many oil pumps on the horizon. The spectacular view included a canyon floor covered in intricate shadows, where cowboys roamed the area organizing cows and bulls. Further down the canyon, the grass thinned out and became a tapestry of rocks. Rebekah called her mother to let her know that they were safe and enjoying their ride through the fields and mountains. It was getting late, but they decided to stop at the canyon stream on their way back.

Alexander appreciated the respect Rebekah showed her mom. He liked that they were traveling through the dark with a full moon paving the way. Their memorable adventure was moving at a nice pace. They made their way down a rocky hill to a small, clear stream where they dismounted in a fenced area to rest their horses and have a drink themselves. This is where the cowboys took shelter; they would kneel, cup their hands, drink from the fresh spring water, then fill up their water bottles.

After a short rest, the three donned their backpacks, adjusted their shirts and tightened their power-belts as they silently thanked Mr. Z for their special boots and everything he gave them. These boots were extremely comfortable and ideal for mountain climbing.

Rebekah provided them a lot of information about the canyon. That scientists believed it was created when the earth's tectonic layers folded. They watch in amazement as Rebekah pointed out the mountains' many layers that clearly validated the science behind this theory. Alexander took out his binoculars and studied the cliffs closely. His attention focused on a section of the cliff where several large rocks protruded in an irregular formation. As he watched he noticed a sculpture in the shape of a Sphinx. He closed his eyes and tried to remember where he had seen that figure before. He checked again and was sure that the Sphinx was carved into the mountain.

"Maxwell," he erupted breathlessly, "do you see the Sphinx in the rocks over there?" he pointed.

"No," Maxwell responded, "I don't see anything." He craned his neck but still shook his head. Alexander gave the binoculars to Rebekah, who also didn't see anything. She shrugged, "I thought I saw an animal's head, but I don't see it anymore."

Alexander bit his lips, remembering Professor Silversmith's lectures about people who were empowered. Could it be possible that he was one of them and could see things that only those who were empowered could? He wondered if Rebekah was also one of them. He grabbed his binoculars and looked again. Now he was sure. This was an impressive sight and he felt drawn to it. And he thought he saw it look right at him and wink.

He noticed something move towards the Sphinx. He looked harder through his binoculars and saw that it was two men in yellow overalls coming out from behind the rock. They weren't visible for a moment, then one of them came out of the shadows waving a yellow flag. Were they sending him a signal? Were they saying, 'Come up here'?

Alexander didn't say anything more to Rebekah and Maxwell but was determined to look into it. He had become a true explorer and enjoyed nothing more than climbing rocks. He did a lot of that behind his home with his dog, Pluto.

Rebekah was happy to be with her two friends. She enjoyed the boys' company and had been laughing and snapping pictures of them all day. She often asked Alexander to take pictures of her and Maxwell as she couldn't wait to show them to Christiana. Alexander was a good photographer and Rebekah jumped for joy when she saw many great shots of her and Maxwell.

Alexander wanted to talk to Maxwell but couldn't see either of the others in the dark. Neither could he see the two men in the distance. He walked a few minutes and noticed more rock formations and several mountain ridges rising up. The mountain spikes to the southwest threw long shadows on to the canyon and the cliffs. Alexander saw a long shadow reach up the cliff to just about where he had spotted the two men. He looked at his watch; it was late evening, so it wasn't the sun that threw the shadows. He picked up his binoculars and was surprised to see shadows from the opposite mountain peak create a shadow of a big arrow pointing to the exact place where the men had stood. No way, he thought, and stopped walking to look through his binoculars.

"What are you looking at?" Maxwell asked coming up behind him.

"I saw some people up there on the mountain," Alexander pointed. Maxwell pulled out his binoculars and looked.

"Yes, I see them," he shouted and saw where the big arrow was pointing. Alexander looked again but he didn't see the men now. They decided to climb up the mountain to that area. Rebekah also tried several times but couldn't see anything. Then with her naked eyes she saw the two men move fast and disappear behind the rocks. She froze and called out,

"I see them – yes I see them - there they are!" she pointed.

They kept looking, but the men disappeared again. Alexander noticed the arrow had moved too. They continued their climb and eventually arrived at the area.

"Could be smugglers? Maxwell wondered aloud, "we might be on to something big, a conspiracy," he continued.

"Yes, something is strange," Rebekah agreed.

"Let's find out; after all we are the musketeers," Maxwell gushed, and raised his left arm.

They all lifted their left arms and pumped their clenched fists into the air, calling out in unison:

"ONE FOR ALL AND ALL FOR ONE!"

The Mysterious Cavern

The three explorers climbed up the steep cliffs until they reached a small ridge where they sat and rested. They were really grateful to Mr. Z for giving them the tools to become such incredible explorers. Right now, it was the magic sneakers they really appreciated. They prevented slipping, were light and comfortable and made them feel secure.

Alexander kept looking through his binoculars checking for the two men in yellow overalls. "There! There! Do you see the yellow flag?" he pointed, and Rebekah and Maxwell nodded that they did indeed see it!

They raced up the hill and came to a tree formation a number of yards away. They thought they had found their target. They maneuvered over to the trees and found a narrow opening to the cave entrance. It seemed as if the rocks had cracked open deep into rock, probably caused by the earth's movements.

"They could be inside this cave," Rebekah suggested. The boys agreed. Alexander, being the smallest of the three, offered to climb over the rock to look. It was a steep drop, so they attached a mountain-climber's rope to his belt. Rebekah and Maxwell held tightly to the end. Alexander climbed into the narrow hole with knife in hand, ready to defend himself. It was moist and slippery inside, but after going in several yards, a pyramid-shaped cave opened up. It was filled with skins that looked as if they came from reptiles although he didn't see any snakes. There were narrow cracks in the walls of the cave, but no sign of the men.

Rebekah left Maxwell to hold the rope and went to get her binoculars. She came back and scanned the surroundings. She saw green areas covered with plush trees that formed into a V-shape. Suddenly she saw something move behind the trees and was surprised to see a man crawling into the open. The person was dressed in camouflage and had green leaves covering his head, the better to blend into the natural surroundings. A few minutes later, she saw a second man. Then an arm grabbed something and pulled it back. The item was yellow. Rebekah held her spot so she wouldn't be discovered, then the camouflaged figure pulled back and disappeared from sight.

She wondered if they were smugglers or maybe spies. She suggested as much to Maxwell, and when Alexander showed up she told him about her observation.

"Definitely drug smugglers," said Maxwell somewhat uneasy.

"Let's get them," Alexander said, all excited.

They donned their backpacks and equipment and began to climb toward the V-shaped tree formation. They moved fast until they reached a point that ended at a steep cliff and they didn't think they could go past it. They were looking for a solution when Alexander had a plan. He saw some rock spires on the top of the steep cliff, so he took off his power-belt and lassoed it to the rope which he threw up to the pointed rocks. It failed on the first few tries, but he kept trying and it finally attached to the spire. He gave the rope a good pull to make sure it was secure and with his backpack secure he started to climb. Maxwell followed and Rebekah tied the rope securely to her waist after which the two boys pulled her up. Once at the top they could easily climb over the rocks.

*   *   *

THE SECRET CAVE

"It looks different," Rebekah noticed, "it looks as if the pointed rock has moved," she continued. They all agreed but there was still no trace of the two men.

"Smugglers for sure," whispered Maxwell.

"It could be," agreed Alexander, shaking his head as he looked down and said, "Did they move the rock to confuse us? Do they have such superhuman powers?" They wondered about all this as they began climbing down, until they passed the rock that had blocked their way. They then approached the green V-bush tree formation from the other side and when they reached beyond this rock, they again attached a climbing-rope to a pointed rock and descended down the cliff to a platform not too far from the trees. The rocks were moist and slippery; a sign that there was water under the ground that allowed the trees to flourish.

Rebekah's telephone rang. "Hey mom," she

answered. "We're having a great time. We're climbing cliffs and exploring caves," she continued. "Yes, mom, we're careful," Rebekah said, and hung up.

Alexander and Maxwell found the mouth of the suspicious cave which was surrounded and partially blocked by the trees. Alexander led the team into the cave and when they reached a fork, Maxwell went to the right and Alexander and Rebekah to the left.

A few minutes later they heard the walkie-talkie on their phones explode in their ears.

"It's a blind cave here," Maxwell breathed with alarm into the phone, "I'm coming back!"

He wasn't really sure, but it looked as if it was a dead end. He turned back and caught up with the other two explorers. The cave was too wet, and rocks were loose and dropping around them, which appeared to cause some openings. Rebekah and Alexander continued to search the area for secret chambers where the smugglers might be hiding. They passed old snakeskins and skeletons of reptiles the further they went. Rebekah fell behind and used the walkie-talkie to keep in touch with the boys.

"Hi guys, I've heard it said," she laughed, "that snakes eat themselves. I think this is proof of that."

"Yeh, right," Alexander answered her. They all met up a few yards later and moved further down the cave, which was so slippery that they decided it would be safer to tie their climbing rope to each other. Rebekah moved ahead of the boys and lengthened the rope so she could move faster, when suddenly she screamed.

"Oh my God, Yikes!!".

"Are you okay?" they called over the walkie-talkies.

"No," she responded. "I just saw an ugly salamander or a crocodile that looked more like a monster. Get me out of here!!!" she screamed.

They pulled her back carefully and Alexander changed places with her and became the leader. He moved down to a lower level where it was drier. He saw more animal skeletons but no sign of the two men. Rebekah and Maxwell were joined to him by the rope, so they moved closer to each other.

As they descended, the cave got wider. They came to another landing and the cave darkened so they took out their power stick and opened up its flashlight. The light exploded into the cave and they could see everything as clear as daylight. Maxwell saw a shining object, a bright gold color metal so they all went to look more closely. Alexander was the first to climb further down into the cave.

"They have created some steps. I wonder if they're expecting us?" Alexander yelled back. Rebekah followed him closely.

"Maybe it's a trap?" she said.

Next, Maxwell descended; they were all down at the bottom. The shining gold material didn't look real, so they were disappointed.

This wasn't the end of their descent. They saw that the cave went further down. Alexander led the group. It was even wetter and more slippery down there. Even though they were connected with the security rope Alexander told them both to keep their walkie-talkies out. Using his amazing wand, the light in the cave made it easy to see where they were going. Then Alexander noticed another landing and the opening to another cave.

He checked his amazing compass and reported, "This entrance is to the south, about 168 degrees." Rebekah and Maxwell continued to move in that direction.

"Wow, this is getting more and more exciting," observed Maxwell into the walkie-talkie.

"Yeah, but it's quite late and we should think about going back now," responded Rebekah. Alexander was too excited about what was going on and ignored the time. With the light from their amazing wand lighting up the cave they didn't realize that it was dark outside, and he went into the opening of the next cave without responding to Rebekah.

"It is beginning to get harder down here," Alexander warned. He felt hampered by the rope on his belt, so he decided to untie it, although he did hold it in his hand, so he didn't lose contact with the others. He then jumped down into the steep shaft.

The cave was filled with rock formations that looked like banking boxes and which formed tables and chairs. It was kind of strange. Looked like a wizard might have created it.

He described it to the others and warned them to be careful because it was even more slippery down there.

But their amazing boots were sturdy and allowed them to move easily on the difficult terrain.

"Oh my God, it looks amazing." Alexander called back. Suddenly he found himself falling. He landed on his behind but landed on his knapsack and found himself being pulled down into a twisted-tube cave by the force of gravity. He fought to get control but couldn't stop sliding... faster and faster, as if he was on a water slide. He was bobsledding on his knapsack.

Faster and faster he moved into a twisting tunnel. As the air got heavier he nearly lost his hat, then he slowed a little, saw a large opening and found himself flying out of the tunnel. Whew!!! He landed on a stack of hay and leaves that buffered his fall and he didn't get hurt.

Alexander was confused then thought he saw Mr. William Harkens' face wink at him!

"Where am I?" he thought but looking up he did see a huge copy of William Marshall Harkens portrait and it really was winking at him. He knew now that he was expected here, and that someone had made sure he would have a soft landing.

Alexander smiled and looked around in awe. It seemed as if it was early morning. He wondered if they had been exploring the caves all night. He wasn't tired and he wondered if their families were worried. But he ignored these thoughts. The trees and plants were exotic looking, with the cliff walls covered in ivy... or at least it looked like ivy. Then he saw a welcoming Sphinx carving on the rocks...

* * *

BACK IN THE GREEN CAVERN

Meanwhile Maxwell was calling out louder and louder to Alexander, "Alex, are you okay? Alexander, are you there?" Rebekah was getting irritated. "Stop yelling and use the walkie-talkie you silly boy." She pulled out her walkie-talkie, "Alexander, do you read me? Alexander, do you read me?" But all she could hear was raspy sounds that were impossible to make out. It was a swishing noise or maybe heavy wind. She looked at Maxwell, raised her left hand with a closed fist and yelled, "One for all and all for one!"

He looked at her and nodded, "Of course, we're like the army, we leave no man behind," Maxwell exclaimed. Rebekah smiled then pulled on the rope and found that Alexander wasn't on the end of it. Now she was really worried. She pulled it back and made sure that she and Maxwell were connected with their rope. She then moved aggressively through the cave, staying in walkie-talkie contact with Maxwell who followed closely down the steep tunnel.

"Wow, Alexander was right," Maxwell heard Rebekah say, when she saw the wizardly cave with rock formations in the form of chairs and tables. They looked welcoming, like someone was expecting company.

When Maxwell was beside her he took out his compass and, seeing that it pointed south, they moved quickly toward the south end of the cave. He found the steps leading to the next cave, the one Alexander had mentioned over his radio. Rebekah lifted her flashlight, which gave her a full view, and using her rope she descended slowly and carefully. Maxwell followed her and she soon reached the more slippery cave. But their shoes kept them safe as they moved.

"Be careful Max," she warned as she continued into the cave.

"Yes, I see," he said.

"Bend forward and balance like when you're skiing." Then suddenly he heard "Oooh!!! oooh!!!" as Rebekah screamed.

"Are you okay? Are you...? Oooh-wow!!!" he was dragged into the tunnel and they both began a very fast slide sitting on their backpacks, as Alexander had done. Rebekah and Maxwell slid down the winding path so fast that they almost lost their breath. The roller coaster ride continued for a while with increasing speed. Rebekah was really scared and continued yelling and kicking her legs in an effort to stop the slide.

Meanwhile, at the other end of the tunnel...

Alexander cleaned up. He removed the mud from his boots so that they shone again, and he could see his name engraved on them. He rearranged his explorer uniform and adjusted all the paraphernalia.

He was walking around an enormous green park when he heard Rebekah's loud scream coming from the tunnel and turned towards the tunnel to see her shoot out and land on the soft hay. She was definitely upset and yelling bloody murder.

"Hey, hey, hey," Alexander called out, "calm down, calm down."

She turned her head, saw that she was safe and Maxwell came flying out and landed next to her. They both looked shocked.

They saw Alexander bent over with laughter.

He went over and helped them to their feet. They dusted the dirt off their clothes and looked around.

"Where are we Alexander?" Rebekah asked.

"I have no idea," smiled Alexander, shaking his head, "but I feel very safe."

"It's such a beautiful place. I wonder what we'll find here," Rebekah said with a smile.

Maxwell asked somewhat sadly, "Do you think we'll find our way home?"

*　　*　　*

Dear Reader. You'll have to read Book 2 to learn what happens to the Musketeers.

Biography

Niels H. Lauersen, M.D., Ph.D.

Dr. Lauersen had a more than 40-year career as a world-renowned Park Avenue surgeon; a New York-based obstetrician/gynecologist and fertility expert, who gave the gift of a child to thousands of families. He taught at many of New York's world-famous medical schools and was the author of more than 14 women's health-related books and hundreds of medical articles. His reputation exploded with appearances on Phil Donahue, Oprah, Regis and Kathy Lee, Charlie Rose, Geraldo Rivera, Sally Jessie Raphael, Maury Povitch and Nancy Merrill.

He'd seen the world at its best and at its worst. In his twilight years he turned to writing fantasy novels for the young and young-at-heart. His rich imagination will help young people understand good and evil and his books are dedicated to entertaining and helping spark their creativity.

www.ingramcontent.com/pod-product-compliance
Lightning Source LLC
Chambersburg PA
CBHW050740230626
47052CB00004BA/762